# THE ALIEN WITHIN

Book Two of
The Alien Chronicles

Robin Martin

Published by Bennett Lane Press 2017



www.robinmartinthomas.com



A catalogue record for this book is available from the National Library of Australia.

Book cover design and formatting services by bookcovercafe.com

ISBN:
978-0-9946465-2-1 (pbk)
978-0-9946465-3-8 (e-bk)

To Auntie Jess:

*A good friend and a much better driving
instructor than Zoe's dad!*

# Chapter One

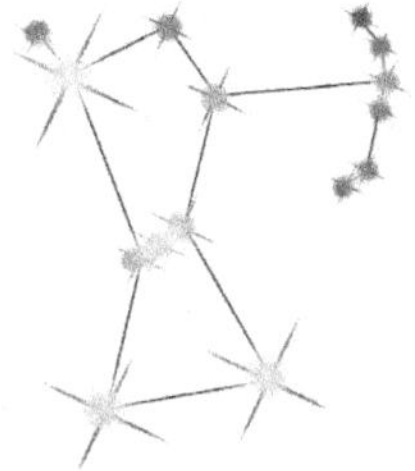

'Oops, so sorry, Zoe. Was that your lunch?'

I looked from where my books had tumbled over the school steps, to my squashed lunch in its brown paper bag, to the black shoe next to it, and finally up to where she stood. Jas's highlighted, blonde hair hardly stirred in the breeze, and her tanned face broke into a phoney smile. Once we'd been friends, but that was ancient history now.

'Yeah, thanks for standing on it, Jas.' I picked up everything and straightened, giving her a scathing look.

She never even batted a fake eyelash. Instead, she just shrugged. 'Total accident. Didn't even see it until it was too late. Never mind. Think of all the carbs I've saved you from. Seriously, I didn't think people ate sandwiches any more. All that bread ... but I guess you don't worry about that sort of thing,' she said, laughing.

Behind her, Chad Everett grinned. Funny, I'd even liked him, too, once.

Then Jas leaned in closer, and I held my books tightly. I didn't want any more 'accidents'. Her blue eyes had that look in them that I remembered so well.

She whispered in my ear, 'Zoe, honey, some friendly advice. When you have long hair, you really need to straighten it, especially if it's frizzy. Personally, I thought you looked cute with a bob last year and it's so much easier to take care of if you have difficult hair. Oh, there's the bell. Catch up later. Byeee!' She turned her back and walked away with a jaunty step.

I gritted my teeth to stop from calling out a totally inappropriate word, which would only have added to her amusement. I wasn't going to give her that satisfaction. As if the first day of year twelve didn't already suck.

I was alone, totally. I'd been alone since the day Rion left last September, but now that I was back at school after a long, unhappy summer, it hit me again. There was no one getting crazily excited about the new stuff we would learn, or how great it would be to plan our university courses for next year. There was no one to lecture me about the benefits of a healthy breakfast or rising early. No one was there to tell me not to worry about my looks, my friends, or who I was going to eat lunch with.

That didn't matter, Rion would say, and besides, we would eat lunch together. In fact, that's how we had done everything—together.

If anyone had told me seven months ago that Rion and I no longer had to be linked, that we could live our separate lives without getting ill (literally) every time we were more than a hundred metres apart, I'd have turned cartwheels. I'd have thought it was better than getting tickets to a Seven Seconds of Summer concert. I'd even have traded in my new learner driver's permit. In short, I would have been ecstatic.

How things change.

Funny to think how much I had hated Rion at first, especially after I found out we were linked for life. But then I got to know him and I discovered he wasn't so bad. Even when we argued, somehow we managed to become closer. And then, just as things were looking promising … he'd left.

I was shattered. It had taken a long time to get over that (along with a lot of tears, litres of chocolate-honeycomb ice cream and several kilometres of red liquorice strips). Finally I had, at least I thought I had. Now, I wasn't so sure.

I was back at school, where Jas and her group hated me, and Harry and his group tolerated me. And even Harry … I hadn't seen him in the months since he'd been sick. I didn't know if we'd still be friends, especially after what happened last year. I didn't know where I stood with anyone anymore. Rion would've helped me work it out, because that's what he did best—help me. But now I was on my own.

I headed for class, and had just reached the door to go in when I collided with a guy who looked vaguely familiar.

'Sorry,' I said, stepping back.

'No worries … oh, hi, Zoe.'

I looked up, recognised who it was and nearly dropped my books again. Jas might be the same, but here was one person who definitely wasn't.

He'd grown a couple of centimetres and all his puppy chubbiness had been replaced by muscle. He had the same smile, and yeah, his eyes and hair were still brown, but other than that, nothing else was familiar. Even his voice had dropped an octave or something.

All I could think was: what had happened to Harry Crosby over the summer? For the first time ever, he was hot, seriously hot.

'Harry?' It was hard for me to believe my eyes. 'You look … different.'

'Yeah, I lost some weight when I was sick last year and then I grew over the summer.' He gave me a tiny smile and added, 'I'm finally taller than you.'

Still finding words difficult, I looked up at his now broad shoulders.

'Anyway, we better get into class. I think we're blocking the door,' he said.

He needn't have worried, because even the people behind us had stopped to look at Harry. In the past they would have brushed past him, but not today. I think there were a couple of open mouths.

He just ignored them as he went inside the classroom. I trailed after him.

'See you at lunch maybe,' he said as he slipped into a seat. 'That is, if you still want to eat with our group.'

Hmm, subtle dig. Very unlike Harry.

Harry and I used to be mates and we had known each other since forever. Our mums even taught at the same primary school. Harry had been short and definitely nerdy. He had often been the butt of the cool kids' jokes, when he was noticed at all. He hadn't cared, much, and that was what I'd liked about him, plus he was really nice. We used to feel so comfortable with each other. Past tense.

Slipping into a seat at the back, I looked again at the transformation that was Harry. Gosh, he even had cheekbones now, and his hair was styled, and just slightly longer. He was like one of those people on a makeover show, and if I hadn't known him so well I would hardly have recognised him.

Last year he'd caught glandular fever and was off school for most of term four. And then it had been the summer holidays. Who would have thought that sickness and a growth spurt could change a person so much? I wondered if he'd still be the same nice guy I used to know, or whether his personality had had a change, too.

At first break, I wandered over to the seats under the shade shelter where Harry and his group sat. Pasting on a smile, I sat down next to them.

'Hey,' I said. I took out the apple, which was now all that was left of my squashed lunch.

Harry looked at me, nodded and then concentrated on taking the lid off his water bottle.

Last year, after Jas's group dropped me, I used to sit with Rion. And it hadn't seemed to matter about anyone else. Then, after Harry had left, I'd started to sit with this group and they'd been too polite to exclude me. It wasn't like I was best buddies with any of them, them, not like I'd been with Harry anyway. But at one time, before Rion and even before Jas, we'd been friends-ish and I'd been in their group.

Lou Kennedy looked at me with her pale blue eyes and moved over a little to give me more room. She gave me a half smile. 'Hi,' she said.

Lou was a girl of few words and I think the only boy she'd ever talked to in her life was Harry. To say she was shy was like saying Taylor Swift was a singer, or that *Master Chef* was a cooking program. She was one of those people that no one ever noticed. Her brown hair often covered her face and her words were mumbled, unless she was speaking to someone she knew well. With us, she was as normal as she ever got.

Kerri, who had an open book beside her, looked up and nodded. She wore a sensible school broad-brimmed hat, even here under the shade because, as she often told us, Queensland had the highest incidences of skin cancer in the world. And with her pale, freckled skin, she said she couldn't take any chances. Kerri and risk taking were not a match.

Harry still said nothing. Yup, looked like the awkwardness between us hadn't disappeared over the summer, even though that fateful family barbecue had been a long time ago.

'So, how was everyone's summer?' I asked, determined to make an effort.

Kerri shrugged. 'I read some of the books on our English list, as well as Zumdahl's *Introductory Chemistry*, and of course *Basic Physics* by Karl Kuhn.

What could I say to that? 'Of course,' I said.

If Rion had been there he would've launched into an in-depth discussion with her. Nothing like that ever had happened between him and me, apart from him nagging me to do my science homework and me flipping him off. Rion and I had had our moments—good and bad.

Harry still said nothing. His silence had seemed to affect everyone.

Finally Lou asked me, 'How was your summer?'

'Okay. I went to visit my gran in Sydney.'

'Sydney, cool,' she said.

'Yeah, it was, especially the Bondi Beach part. What about you?'

'Nothing much, I started tennis lessons …' Her voice trailed off. Lou hated talking about herself.

'Great,' I said politely. 'Tennis sounds like a lot of fun.'

'Mum says it's a great way to meet people.' She flicked her brown hair over her shoulder and went back to her lunch.

Another long stretch of silence.

Kerri returned to her book, and Lou had evidently decided she'd made enough of a contribution to the conversation, but I decided to give it one more try. After all, Harry did suggest I join them.

'So, Harry, what did you do over the holidays?'

'I had a pretty quiet summer,' he said. 'It took me a while to recover from my illness. Then my uncle came back from his holiday in the States and we worked out together for a while. He said it would help me build up my strength again.' He shrugged as if it was no big deal.

He definitely didn't realise how hot he looked. More than one girl had checked him out that morning, but he obviously hadn't noticed. Even Jas had done a double take when she saw him.

And he was eating a *salad*, of all things. The only time I'd ever seen him eat greens was when they were on a big Mac. Despite his mum's best efforts, Harry had been a confirmed junk-food addict.

'Your uncle, eh? Would that be Adrian, your mum's youngest brother?' I knew Harry's family almost as well as I knew my own.

'Yeah, that's right. He stayed with us over the summer while he was looking for his own place. He's really into fitness and is going to be a personal trainer. He said he would start with me and help me get fit. So we trained together.' He gave me a shy smile, and for a microsecond I glimpsed the old Harry again.

'Well, he did a good job,' I said and smiled back at him. At least we were talking again, even if it was a bit awkward.

'Harry looks great, doesn't he?' Lou said.

I could almost see those stars in her eyes. Oh dear. I hoped Harry would be kind to her. The old Harry would've been, but I wondered about the new one.

'It's really quite simple, isn't it?' Kerri said, speaking at last. She pushed up the glasses that had fallen down her nose. 'If you combine a healthy diet and an exercise program, you're bound to get results. Add to that a growth spurt, which often happens to young males as they mature, and Harry's voice finally breaking, and you have a perfectly logical explanation as to why he looks and sounds different.'

It could have been Rion talking, without the charm. I thought Kerri was headed for a brilliant career in a top university as either a doctor or a scientist. Sadly, her social skills were not quite in the same league, and she had no filters whatsoever.

Harry just smiled. 'You're right, Kerri,' he said.

'I usually am,' she said, and then took another bite of her chicken wrap.

'You look different too, Zoe,' Harry said. 'Your hair …'

'I decided to grow it,' I said.

'It looks … nice.'

'Thanks.'

He was starting to sound like the old Harry again. I wondered if he was finally over what had happened last year. Could we possibly be friends again? I really hoped so.

'Although in this hot weather short hair is more practical,' Kerri said. 'Much cooler.' She pointed to her own red hair peaking out from under her hat. 'You should cut it.'

'I'll keep that in mind,' I said.

Although Kerri and fashion sense were not words I would usually put in the same sentence, I thought she might have a point. Why bother looking good if no one was going to notice? Well, it was true that Jas had noticed my hair, but not in a good way. And Harry had, too, but he was probably just being polite and couldn't think of anything else to say.

'You know, we should go to McDonald's this afternoon,' Lou said out of the blue.

We all looked at her in surprise. That was something this group never did. Lou was usually too shy, Kerri always wanted to go home and study, and Harry hated going places where he might be made fun of. Last year I had mostly been with Rion, and he disapproved of fast food.

'Why?' Kerrie said, her brow furrowing.

Lou shrugged. 'Why not? It's the first day of our last year at school. It might be good to celebrate or something.'

I was beginning to think Harry wasn't the only one who had changed over the summer.

Harry shrugged. 'I guess.'

Lou beamed.

'Aren't you afraid you might get into bad habits and start to eat junk food again? It's a lot easier to put on weight than take it off, you know,' the ever-diplomatic Kerri said.

'I think I'll be safe with a diet cola or a coffee,' Harry said, trying not to smile. 'What about you, Zoe?'

'Sure,' I said. I was curious about how this new Harry would interact with the others now that he was, had to say it, hot.

So the afternoon went by a little quicker than the morning. I actually had something to look forward to—at least I hoped I did, anyway. I knew Jas, Chad, Chelsea and the rest of that group would probably be at Macca's. Would they still pay Harry out? Or maybe I'd be the new target.

Macca's was a short walk from our school. It was well placed; it got most of its customers, as well as its staff, from the students at our high school. Not me, though. I wasn't allowed to work there, or anywhere else, while I was at school. My parents (ever optimistic) wanted me to concentrate on my studies. My pocket money usually came from babysitting jobs and odd chores I did around the house, so I didn't have heaps of money, but it would stretch to a cheeseburger. And today I was feeling hungry; after all, someone had stepped on my lunch.

Jas and her groupies were sitting at the corner table as usual. It had a prime view of who was coming and going, and it was in the best position to feel the full effect of the air-conditioning. Chad had his arm around Jas, and Chelsea was leaning in close to talk to her.

Their table erupted with laughter and several glances were directed my way. I had a pretty good idea what they were talking about. And who.

Ignoring them, I scanned the room and saw Lou with an outstretched arm, waving to me. Beside her were Harry and Kerri. I guessed Kerri thought she could forego studying for once, since it was the first day back. I went over to join them.

'Hey, this is cool, isn't it?' Lou said, giggling.

'Yeah, literally.' I sat down, enjoying the air-conditioning after the thirty-plus degrees outside.

Lou just looked at me blankly, but Harry grinned. Good to know we were still on the same wavelength at times.

Seeing their drinks on the table, I realised they'd already ordered. 'I might get a burger, I didn't have much lunch today,' I said, getting up again.

Harry said, 'I'll come, too. I could do with another coffee.'

We walked over to the queue, which wasn't far from Jas's table. As we waited to order, she got up and, swinging her blonde hair over her shoulders, headed towards us. I tried not to let my jaw drop.

Ignoring me, she smiled sweetly at Harry and said, 'Wow, Harry, look at you, all grown up and everything.'

Harry said nothing. I could tell he was as surprised as me.

Jas laid a hand on his arm. 'You know, whatever it was you did this summer, you should keep on doing it because it's working. Chelsea is just dying to find out all about it. Why don't you come over and join us?'

If someone had told me last year that Jas would ever invite Harry Crosby over to her group, I would've thought they were insane or pulling my leg. No way would it have happened, ever. It would be like winning Gold Lotto or something, the chances were that slim. I looked up at Harry, wondering what he would say.

'Thanks, Jas, but I'm sitting with Zoe and some of our other friends. However, Chelsea is welcome to join us, if she wants to—and you.'

I bit my lip to keep from laughing. I wished I could whip out my phone and take a picture of Jas's face. There was a swirl of emotions that went from disbelief, to anger and then a serious attempt at recovery, something she was very good at.

'That's so sweet of you, Harry, but we're with friends, too. Maybe some other time, when you're not so … busy, you can join us. But don't leave it too long.'

After firing her warning shot, she walked back to her group, her blonde hair swinging. Last year she wouldn't have given Harry the time of day. Now, just because he looked good, he had an open invitation to join the beautiful people. But I knew there would be a time limit on that invitation because Jas was not known for her patience.

We got our order and headed back to our table. 'Good on you, Harry,' I said quietly.

He frowned. 'I've never liked Jas or her friends. And I have a good memory, especially for how they treated me in the past. I know who my real friends are.'

As we sat down again, I wondered if that included me

'Was that Jas who came up to speak to you?' Lou asked Harry, wide eyed. 'What did she want?'

'Nothing important,' he said, and took a sip of his coffee.

'Nothing she says ever is,' Kerri said, in a rare perceptive moment. 'You did the right thing in leaving her group last year, Zoe.'

I didn't remind her that I was the one who'd been dropped, not the other way round.

Lou nodded. 'Yeah, you're better off back with us. And now that Harry's back it's just like old times, isn't it?'

Harry gave me a real smile this time and said, 'Yeah, just like old times.'

As I took a bite of my cheeseburger, I thought maybe this year wouldn't be so bad after all.

# Chapter Two

I jumped back on the curb as a loud honk blasted my eardrums and a car rushed past me, missing my toes by a mere 5.6 centimetres. I glared at the vanishing Holden Commodore and then, glancing up at the lights, realised they hadn't changed. How could I have been so careless?

Taking another step back, I waited, the hot February sun beating down on my head. I had forgotten to wear a hat. In the past I never forgot anything, but now … now everything was different, especially me.

I had a secret. No one knew except Zoe Brennan, not that she'd ever tell anyone. She'd probably forgotten about me by now. Besides, she never expected to hear from me again. And she never would. I owed her that.

But in the end I hadn't been able to leave. There were many reasons, but the main one was Zoe. Just to know we breathed the same mix of nitrogen and oxygen, looked up at the same night sky, lived in the same world, was enough for me. I wondered if she ever thought of me when she saw the constellation Orion in the sky.

I had never expected to like her, and at first she certainly didn't like me. We were opposites in every way. Then I discovered that I did like her, and what was even more surprising, I actually learnt from her. I had never anticipated that.

But at least she was free now. And that's what she had wanted since the day we'd first met. Now that she thought I was gone, she could grow up the way she was meant to. It was for the best. Really.

Depression settled over me, something I'd never experienced when I'd been a disembodied, highly intelligent being for four thousand years. This wasn't what I expected when I made the decision to become human several months ago.

I was trying to learn about being human, about being an organic again. I knew my good fortune. I had been given a unique choice: return to my people or stay. I chose the latter, yet inside nothing had changed. Inside, I was still an alien.

It wasn't as though my people had totally abandoned me. I had money and a place to stay—we're good at that sort of thing: organising. Years of having hosts that were bankers, financiers, businessmen and the odd corrupt politician or two had taught us a few things about survival. But I was starting to realise that surviving wasn't living. Living was much harder to do.

Sometimes—actually, most times—I found humans confusing and difficult to understand. I didn't always know what normal was, and I no longer had Zoe to help me work it out. In fact, I think I'd gotten worse with the months of isolation.

The light finally changed and I crossed the street, weaving my way through the stream of people crossing from the opposite side. Why weren't they more orderly? I didn't even bother to work out the answer.

I sought the shade on the other side of the street and stopped to think.

I'd assumed I knew all about being human when I first set out on my own, but I couldn't have been more wrong. I'd had many sleepless nights thinking about Zoe. Sometimes I was tempted to go back. Once, in a moment of weakness, I did go to her house. The light from her bedroom window drew me like a magnet. I'd even bought her favourite treats of hot chips and red liquorice strips. It would've been so easy to call out to her, to tell her I'd made a mistake, especially in leaving her. Everything could go back to the way it was.

Except it wouldn't. I left in the first place so she could be free to live her life as a normal teenager and not be burdened by having a relationship with a 4000-year-old alien. Nothing could change who I was. I might look like a human (actually, as I told Zoe, humans look like us rather than the other way around) but inside I was still an alien. So I turned away from her house and never went back.

Reaching the small unit that had been my home for the last five months, I put my gym gear away, had a shower and then debated whether to continue the game of online chess I'd started yesterday or have lunch. The empty feeling in my stomach told me it was time to prepare food. Despite all my dietary advice to Zoe in the past, I hadn't been careful with my own diet. Another first for me.

Opening the freezer door, I took out a small, ready-made meal to put in the microwave. I knew I needed to start preparing healthy meals. And I would, once I worked out a calorie-controlled, balanced diet for one. In the meantime, fast food was just so … fast.

Seven minutes and forty-six seconds later, as I placed the lasagne on a plate, there was a knock on the door.

This was unusual for two reasons. Firstly, no one had ever knocked on my door before. Secondly, I didn't know anyone.

Surely it couldn't be …

It wasn't Zoe. Instead, a middle-aged man of medium height, a perfect BMI and a serious expression stood there.

'Greetings, Rion,' he said, 'how have you been?'

I recognised the being. He had materialised several months ago in order to 'rescue' me from Zoe's family by pretending to be my uncle.

Using the human name he had chosen, I said, 'Archimedes? What are you doing here? I thought you'd returned to the mothercloud.'

He crossed his arms over his chest and gave me a level stare from his grey eyes. 'I did, but it was felt your need was greater than mine. You need a guardian, so I was sent back. Aren't you going to invite me in?'

Too surprised to say anything, I opened the door so he could pass. He walked in and stood in the middle of the flat, looking around, shifting his gaze from the tiny kitchenette at one end to the living area at the other. I was suddenly uncomfortably aware of my breakfast dishes, which I'd washed but left stacked in the dish rack, and the steaming lasagne on a plate.

Bending down, he ran a finger along the top of the coffee table, where I hadn't dusted. He picked up a sock (clean) that had fallen from the laundry basket on the opposite chair and dropped it back in. Brushing some crumbs off the black vinyl sofa, he sat down.

'I came as quickly as I could,' he said, looking at me with a frown, 'but not a moment too soon, by the look of things.'

Lifting the laundry basket off the chair, I sat down. My bottom sank into a deep crevice and my knees nearly touched my chin. This chair, which I only used for storing things, clearly hadn't been designed for any human frame I'd ever seen. I was feeling at a distinct disadvantage. I waited for him to speak, realising I was being assessed.

He scanned me with his perfect 20/20 vision, which was enhanced by his ability to determine height, weight and other physical factors within seconds.

'You've put on 2.65 kilograms, and that's mostly fat, not muscle. Your skin has an unhealthy tan, which means you've been getting too much sun. You also have dark circles under your eyes, which could indicate a medical condition that needs investigating. Either that, or you're not getting adequate sleep. You do realise you have an organic existence now and have to behave accordingly, right?'

I was beginning to feel like something under a microscope. Defending myself, I said, 'I've been doing regular exercise and have had sufficient nutrients. It's sometimes difficult to maintain a balanced diet when cooking for one.'

My words sounded stilted, even to me, the way I'd first sounded when I became human. It was a lame attempt to excuse my dietary habits and I knew it. But I continued, determined not to let him get to me.

'Also, a certain amount of sunshine is necessary for vitamin D. Perhaps, though, I do need to investigate my sleeping patterns.' I certainly wasn't going to tell him I wasn't sleeping well because I was thinking about Zoe. I could just imagine his reaction to that. Not good.

'Your unsatisfactory diet and sleeping habits need to be remedied immediately. Being human is dangerous enough without accelerating the problems. And I've made another observation. Your standard of hygiene is not what it should be.' He looked around the room again.

'My standards are very high. I clean quite regularly, and my personal hygiene is extremely thorough. I floss every day.' I was starting to get annoyed. A few misplaced items and some crumbs didn't mean I was grubby. Zoe had often told me I was a 'neat freak'. Perhaps I wasn't quite as tidy as in the past, but I was certainly clean.

'We won't debate those issues now. There are more important things to discuss.' Archimedes sat back and crossed his legs. 'We've noticed that you haven't been using your time wisely in constructive pursuits. Playing games on the computer and watching TV is not what we expected when you chose a human life.'

'I've been playing online chess, a game highly conducive to developing thinking strategies. I've also been learning Mandarin Chinese. And I've been analysing a television series to enable me to interact with humans more successfully.' Archimedes made me feel like a mere youngster of a thousand years or so.

He waved a hand dismissively. 'You need to go back to school.'

'You know that's unnecessary. I've accumulated more knowledge than any human on the planet.'

'If you're going to be a human you have to live like one. You're perceived to be seventeen years old and therefore underage. You need to finish school and attain a qualification that will enable you to get a job and provide for yourself. Surely you've thought of these things.'

'Yes, of course, but I thought I could go straight to university. I was giving myself some time to think about this.'

'Time is up,' Archimedes said, leaning forward and snapping his fingers in front of my face. 'As you're underage you need a guardian, and that is me. I will be looking after you.'

That alarmed me. Archimedes wouldn't have been my choice of an ideal companion.

'You can't do that,' I said. 'If you materialise for too long it'll be difficult for you to transform back into the pure-conscious entities of our people. That's what caused my problems in the first place. Are you telling me you want to be human, too?'

He gave a visible shiver. 'Certainly not, I find this physical form limiting and tiring. I'm making a sacrifice for you, that's true, but not the ultimate one. The very thought of becoming human on a permanent basis fills me with horror. But we have been working on the process of materialising in order to prevent problems of the very sort that landed you in this dilemma in the first place.

'We have discovered that the maximum time we can remain organic without being adversely affected is three hours. So that means, if I dematerialise before that time I can regain my former, more perfect state of existence. Then, when required, I can materialise again. While I will be your guardian in terms of human requirements, it will only be for short periods of time. That will be sufficient to keep up the pretence that you have a human guardian.'

He looked at the analogue clock on the wall. 'And now I have approximately two hours, twenty-eight minutes and forty-two seconds left before I go.' He looked at me with a pleased expression. 'Forty-one now. We can do a lot in that time.'

'So you'll only be with me for short periods.' I felt a surge of relief.

'Did I not just say that? I really do fear for your intelligence now that you've been tainted by human life. It seems to have had a detrimental effect on you.'

Archimedes was a millennium older than my superior and myself, but I was beginning to think that a little more humility on his part wouldn't go amiss.

'So, what's the plan?' I said, just a little impatiently.

'First of all, we need to find more suitable accommodation. I can't be expected to live here, even in the brief times I'll be with you.' He looked around the small unit with distaste. 'I need a temperature-controlled environment and one that's clean.'

I let that last comment slide, but I had to explain to him my choice of home. I got the feeling Archimedes wasn't very practical.

'Accommodation is expensive and I've had to keep within the allowance allotted to me. There weren't a lot of options. Renting has its complications. I had to forge some necessary documents, including a birth certificate. It was only because this unit had been empty for so long that the owner decided to let me have it on a month-by-month basis.'

Archimedes waved a hand airily. 'Your allowance has been increased now that I'm responsible for you. I've already arranged for us to live in a house close to the area where your uncle was supposed to reside.'

'But that's in the neighbourhood where my original host lives,' I said, panicking.

'I fail to see the relevance of that statement,' Archimedes said, in a bored voice.

'Zoe thinks I've returned to our people. She doesn't know I've stayed human.' For someone who had lived nearly five thousand years, Archimedes wasn't showing a lot of wisdom.

He shrugged. 'You'll just have to explain to her that you've changed your mind. Or I could alter her memory. A small thing, but it might make matters more convenient. Yes, I think that would be best overall. I'll arrange it.'

I looked at him and considered. Did I really want Zoe to forget who I was? Forget all the times we'd been together and the friendship we'd had? Did I want her to forget that I'd kissed her three times? Well, to be accurate, twice, because the second time she had kissed me. Yes, it would make things easier but …

'Let me think about it,' I said.

'Don't take too long to decide, because if I remove her memory of you I'll have to do it before you see her again.

I'll return tomorrow to enrol you at the local high school, East Valley High.'

'I can't go there. That's where Zoe and her friends are. They know me.'

'Do her friends know who or what you are? Surely you were not so unwise as to tell them.' Archimedes frowned.

'Of course not—only Zoe knows I'm an alien—but they'll remember me. You might be able to take away her memories, but you can't take away the memories of the whole school.'

'Not necessary,' he said. 'I'll ensure that Zoe forgets you're an alien and the memories associated with that, but she will still remember you as Rion. She'll think what everyone else thinks; that you stayed with her family for a few months before your uncle came and took you with him on one of his trips. That's the wisest course of action.'

'Can't I simply enrol in another school?'

'No, the next school is quite a distance away, and you wouldn't be in what they call the catchment area. I have looked into this, you know.' He gave me another frown.

I said nothing. I wasn't feeling good about this at all.

'Now, gather your possessions and we'll leave,' he continued. 'While I'm waiting, you may get me some filtered water. The day is very warm.' He sighed. 'I hate these physical needs. And do make sure it's in a glass that has been cleaned.'

I wondered if I had been this irritating to Zoe when I first met her.

Nearly two hours later I dropped my bag in the main living area of a spartan, white-walled house. There was a white leather sofa and a glass table with uncomfortable-looking chairs, but little else.

Archimedes flicked on the air-conditioning. 'I arranged for a few essential furnishings on an earlier visit. Providing you maintain the present standard of hygiene and don't clutter the place with superfluous items, I can exist here for short periods of time.'

I opened one of the kitchen cupboards, which was bare. I was guessing Archimedes didn't think dishes and cutlery were necessary. Hopefully, he had thought about acquiring a bed for me.

'It must be nearly time for you to dematerialise, Archimedes,' I said. I would be more comfortable on my own, and there was also some shopping to do.

'Yes, you're correct. I am extremely fatigued. We'll talk again in the morning when I return, and in the meantime you should think about what I said. You'll need to make your decision about your former host, Zoe, by then. Once she sees you again it'll be too late to remove her memories. I need to do it beforehand.'

I watched him close his eyes, his brow furled in concentration. Slowly he faded, becoming fainter and then translucent. Then he was gone.

I let out the breath I'd been holding, relieved to be on my own again. Archimedes was exhausting to be with. Hopefully, his future visits would be few and far between.

But I had something more important to consider. Finally, after all these months, I was going to see Zoe again. Would I let Archimedes take away her memories of me as an alien? And if he did, what exactly would she remember? What did I want her to remember? My heart rate increased and I felt my temperature rise. Whether or not this was due to anticipation or fear, I wasn't quite sure.

# Chapter Three

I dropped the cheese grater and bent down to pick it up, suddenly remembering another time when that had happened. Rion and I had been making dinner together, and just before that, he had told me, ever so casually, about Jas kissing him. I knew then my friendship with the most popular girl in our school was doomed.

But I also realised something else. Rion was becoming more than just an annoying alien that I was stuck with. We were becoming friends, and I was starting to care for him more than I'd realised.

I didn't always like him, no way. He could be irritating and such a know-it-all sometimes. But then, especially after our first date (bowling, would you believe) we started to click. I smiled to myself as I grated the cheese into a bowl. That was when we 'd had our first kiss. Rion may not have known much about being human back then, but he sure knew how to kiss.

As I added the toppings to the pizza we were having for dinner, I started to remember other things: the first time he materialised and danced with me; the hot-air balloon trip he'd planned for my birthday; the time he had invited himself on my one and only date with Harry Crosby to a family barbecue. That had been a mega disaster, but now I could smile about it, sort of.

All these memories just made me miss him more.

Even though my first day at school hadn't totally sucked, I was feeling down. Rion should have been here with me. He should have been encouraging me to study when I was trying to get him to watch Netflix with me instead. He should have been telling me not to eat those Sara Lee brownies—yet he always took one if I offered.

A big, fat, stupid tear rolled down my cheek and plopped onto the kitchen bench. I wiped my eyes with my sleeve and put the pizza in the oven, closing the door with a bang. I was over all this remembering. I might as well study, I decided, because at least reading about the causes of World War I would make me bored rather than miserable thinking about Rion.

Later that night, after dinner and another futile attempt to study, I was still feeling edgy and restless. I thought going for a run might help. Putting on my running shoes, and grabbing my phone and earphones, I slipped out of the house quietly into a still warm twilight. A light breeze was blowing, and the sound of cicadas filled the air.

The light faded from the sky as I jogged down the quiet suburban streets. I knew it was time to put all this behind me. Knowing Rion had been the most incredible experience I'd ever had, and he was the most amazing being I'd ever met, even though he wasn't human. I'd never forget him, but he wasn't coming back and it was time I accepted that.

This could be a good year. Lou and Kerri had finally accepted me, and even Harry seemed to be more normal with me now. I would study hard, maybe even work out what I wanted to do next year. It was my final year of high school. I shouldn't waste it.

After twenty minutes or so, I found myself in an unfamiliar neighbourhood. It was time I turned back. Looking over at the small complex of new townhouses, where a few lights twinkled, my eyes caught the silhouette of a figure in an upstairs window. I stopped and took out my earphones. My pulse quickened, and a queasy but excited feeling fluttered inside me.

I couldn't see the figure clearly, but it seemed familiar. Could it be? The seconds stretched as I looked up, wishing what I wanted to be true. Then whoever it was moved away from the window and the light went out. I waited for a few moments, not really sure what I was waiting for. I sensed … something.

So much for putting it all behind me. I see someone in a window and my imagination goes crazy. Putting in my earphones again, I turned and ran back down the street.

The house had been as bare as I suspected. At least Archimedes had bought a bed, though he evidently thought sheets and pillows were an unneeded luxury. Yet I had to admit this place was a definite improvement on the small, stuffy unit I'd been living in. Once I added a few personal touches, it would be very comfortable, and I'd only have to put up with Archimedes for short periods of time.

I had already stocked the fridge and cupboard with a few necessary items from the local shop. All the while I'd been out, I'd kept a lookout for people I might know. Until I got my story straight, it was going to be awkward seeing anyone from my previous life.

Archimedes said I should tell everyone I had just returned from the Amazon rainforest with my uncle, where he'd had an important project as a photojournalist, and I was going to complete year twelve. That was fine, as far as it went. But what was I going to do about Zoe?

I had an important decision to make. Would I ask Archimedes to take away her memories of me or not? He'd said that the only memory he would remove was her knowledge that I was an alien, but what exactly did that mean?

I went upstairs to get my laptop. The night had set in, my favourite time. I went over to look out the window, searching for the constellation Orion. It was where my home planet was, and had also been the inspiration for my name. Strange, I thought, that in all the years since I'd left my planet behind, I'd never missed my family and home as much as I missed Zoe.

When I'd volunteered for the space program on my home planet, I gave up my organic body to become a totally cerebral entity so I could travel more easily through space and time. I was considered an adolescent, and my age was roughly equivalent to seventeen years in Earth terms. It was the perfect age to apply, as I hadn't had the time to develop any close ties, other than with my birth family. Being accepted into the program was as much an honour for them as for me.

I'd never missed having an organic life, because I'd been living through the many human hosts I'd had over the years.

It was a mutually beneficial relationship. We learnt about human life to further our people's knowledge, and humans learnt about—well, everything. It was a symbiotic relationship, beneficial to all.

And then I met Zoe.

Who would have thought that a female aged only fifteen and three-quarters could wreck so much havoc on my previously calm and unemotional existence. She had been so unimpressed by all I had to offer. But most of the great inventions of the world could be attributed to a human that was host to one of my people. Just ask Isaac Newton or Leonardo da Vinci.

But Zoe had cared nothing for that. All she wanted to do was impress some Neanderthal boy called Chad Evert. So, of course, when she baited me I rose to the challenge and materialised into a human body to help her.

Big mistake. I couldn't change back again.

Doing something dumb to impress a female … you'd think I hadn't previously had four thousand years of vicarious existence through others. If it hadn't been so catastrophic, it would have been laughable. Yet, when I was finally given a choice to return to my planet, I stayed. Only time would tell me whether I'd made the right decision.

And now I had another difficult decision to make. Archimedes was probably right. It would be better to erase

Zoe's memory of me as an alien, and the knowledge that we had once shared a tie that was closer than most human beings would ever know.

Looking out the window, it was hard to see the stars. So I flicked off the light and the room filled with darkness. Walking back to the window, my eyes were drawn to movement on the street. A lone figure on the pavement was looking up at the window where I was standing. I felt an elevation in my pulse rate and held my breath.

I couldn't make out her face, but I knew it was Zoe.

Very unscientific, but I had an unshakeable feeling of certainty. I knew her almost as well as I knew myself. I sensed the quickening of her heartbeat, too, which was keeping a rhythm with mine. I could see the rise and fall of her chest as her quick breaths escaped. I felt her eyes on me, looking, searching …

Had she seen me in the window before I turned out the light? Perhaps the bond between us hadn't been totally severed.

I had to go down to her. This was the only thought in my mind as I left the bedroom.

But halfway down the stairs I paused. Was this wise? Once I saw her it would be too late to take away her memories. Was this fair to Zoe?

That was what the rational side of my brain said. But I had discovered a more emotional side that surprised me at times, like now. I wanted to see her, and nothing else mattered, not even commonsense.

So I continued down the stairs and went out into the night. She was gone.

Those few moments of hesitation had saved us both. Perhaps it was for the best. Every reason I'd had for not getting in contact with Zoe remained. It was only my selfish desire to see her again that had made me forget what was right.

I couldn't help feel a crushing disappointment, but despite this, I knew now what my decision had to be.

# Chapter Four

'Stop!'

My hand jerked and hot liquid spilt onto my fingers. 'Ouch,' I said, turning around.

It was Archimedes, of course. He stood there with disapproval written all over his face.

'Give me some warning before you appear like that, Archimedes. I wasn't expecting you so early. What's so urgent?' I blew on my scalded fingers.

'I thought you were going to amend your habits. Green tea is a much healthier choice.'

I remembered saying the same thing to Zoe. Funny how our own words sound so different coming from someone else's mouth. I decided to ignore him, and said instead, 'Why are you here now? It's only six am. School doesn't start for another two and a half hours.'

Archimedes folded his arms and looked at me. 'I need to know what you want done about your former host. Do you want me to remove her memory of you or not? You should follow my advice. It will be better for all concerned.'

'But she'll still have some memory of me, won't she?' I didn't want her to forget that I'd ever existed.

Archimedes gave an impatient wave of his hand. 'Yes, of course,' he said. 'She'll forget you were an alien and that she was your host. What she'll forget are the *feelings*'—he shuddered at the word—'she had for you. She will remember you as a temporarily homeless boy who stayed with her family for a few months and then was taken away by his uncle. Oh, she might remember that you were slightly different, even somewhat annoying. It's so difficult for humans to understand superior beings such as ourselves.'

I thought about it for a moment. This was best, maybe not for me but for Zoe. I'd made my decision, but it was surprisingly hard to say the words. Finally I said, 'Yes. Do it.'

I sat down at the table and lifted my coffee cup, not wanting Archimedes to know that I was upset. He would only see it as a sign of weakness.

He nodded. 'Good. I'll leave you now and materialise at Zoe's home, where I'll remove her memories.'

'You can't do that. What if someone sees you? And what are you going to do to her?' Panic set in. This seemed much more dangerous than I'd thought. I considered changing my mind.

He brushed my concerns aside with another wave of his hand. 'Even though I'll have to materialise, I'll be invisible to her. I'm not without some talents, you know. Then I'll use my highly developed cognitive abilities to search her mind and remove the memories of you as an alien. It's the work of a few moments only. There'll be no harm to her, and she won't even be aware of me. Such work will tire me and I won't be able to enrol you in school today. That will have to wait until tomorrow. I suppose one more day of your indulgent activities of online games and television programs won't matter.'

I ignored that last insulting remark. Zoe was still my chief concern. 'You're certain you can do this, Archimedes? If there's any chance something could go wrong, I don't want you to do it.'

He gave an elaborate sigh and looked at me with an expression of frustration. 'I cannot believe how much you've forgotten about our superior abilities in such a short time. Of course no harm is going to come to your precious host. But I've wasted enough time here. I must be off before she wakes up. I've noticed she's even more slothful than you in that regard.'

I woke up feeling really calm and Zen-like—so different from yesterday, and in fact, most of the summer. Why had I been so miserable and depressed? All that sadness was gone now, and yet … something felt missing. Although the heaviness that had been with me for so long had disappeared and I felt lighter, I also felt empty.

I looked over at the bright sunlight streaming through the window. I had zero reasons to feel down about anything. Yet something had been upsetting me the last few months. Was it the fact that Harry and I had fallen out last year and I had no close friends anymore? Maybe that was part of it, but not everything. There was something else, something that had made me feel lost. And now it was gone. Weird.

I shook my head as if to clear it. I couldn't work it out. Everything was okay. Not great, but not terrible either. I wasn't down anymore, but I did feel different in some way.

I got up and went over to the cupboard to get my uniform. Then I looked down at the carpet where my history notes from class were scattered. I was almost certain I'd left them on my desk. I picked them up, put them back on the desk and went over to close the window.

The air was still and calm, not even the hint of a breeze. Maybe it had been windy during the night.

Shaking my head again at the strangeness of the morning, I got dressed and surprised Mum and Dad by having breakfast with them, and then I caught the school bus on time for a change. Things were looking up.

Kerri was in my chemistry class, which was a plus because I could get homework answers from her if I was stuck.

And Harry actually spoke two sentences to me in English class.

'So, Zoe, are you going to this play Ms Dawson wants us to see?'

I shrugged. 'Shakespeare? I dunno.'

He nodded. 'Yeah, not my thing either.'

He turned back to open his book as Ms D came into class. It wasn't much in the way of conversation, but at least it was a start.

And speaking of Harry, he sure was attracting attention, especially from the girls. But it was nice to see that it didn't seem to be turning his head. At lunchtime he still sat with us, even though Jas pointedly asked him to sit with her group.

'So Harry, still slumming it, I see,' she said, as she passed our group. 'Oh, no offence, girls,' she added, giving us a nasty smile. 'But you can sit with us, Harry.'

Harry just said, 'These are my friends, so I'll stay here thanks.'

Jas shrugged. 'Up to you.' And she walked away, more than a little annoyed. I sensed that Harry wouldn't get any more invitations from her.

'You can sit with them if you want,' Lou said. I knew she was hoping he wouldn't.

'Nah,' he said. 'I might catch something.'

Lou gave him a puzzled look. 'Like what?'

'Oh, I don't know, maybe a serious case of being up yourself with symptoms of wankyness.' He said it with a straight face but then broke out into a grin.

We all laughed. I was surprised. This was a side of Harry I'd never seen before. He'd never really had the confidence to make jokes, especially sarcastic ones.

'So,' he continued, 'anybody for McDonald's this afternoon?' Another surprise.

Kerri shook her head. 'I really need to get into this chemistry homework. I can't afford to get behind if I want to get into pre-med next year.'

As if. I don't think Kerri ever dropped below an A in her entire school life. She would probably have had like a nervous breakdown or something if she did.

Lou, looking like a sad puppy, said, 'I can't make it either 'cause I've got a tennis coaching session.'

Poor Lou was one of the most uncoordinated people I knew, but her mother still insisted on her doing some kind of sport every year. I think her mum was hoping it would make Lou more social. Lou was onto about her tenth sport now, and not one of them so far had made her less shy or more athletic.

Harry looked over at me. 'What about you, Zoe?'

I hesitated. That would mean just Harry and me going to Macca's. I told myself it wasn't like it was any kind of date or anything, because it would've been our group if the others were going, but it would still look like one.

My last 'date' with Harry had been spectacularly unsuccessful, but that was a long time ago now. We'd both changed. And anyway, this could be my opportunity to get back on a friendly basis with him. I might not have wanted him as a boyfriend, but I kind of missed him as my friend.

'Sure, why not,' I said. 'I've got nothing on this afternoon.'

He nodded, not seeming to care one way or the other. I guessed he must've gotten over his crush on me from last year. So that was good, wasn't it?

After school, we met at the gates and walked to Macca's together. We talked about school and stuff like we'd always done over the years. And that was the thing. I'd known Harry for as long as I could remember and we were comfortable with each other. At least we used to be. Now it seemed things were getting back to normal, sort of.

For once Jas and her friends weren't hanging out at their usual table.

'Wow, no Jas and co,' I said, as we swung through the glass doors.

'Yeah,' Harry said, 'bet the profits will be down for the day.'

We laughed together as we lined up to order. Then, taking our diet colas, we headed over to a seat in the corner.

'You know, I still can't get over how you've changed,' I said.

'Only on the outside, Zoe,' he said. 'I'm still me.'

'Yes and no, you've changed a little on the inside, too. You're more confident. You'd never have come to Macca's with me before. You used to say it wasn't your thing.'

He shrugged. 'Maybe I don't feel so awkward anymore, that's true. I guess Uncle Adrian helped a lot there. He made me feel like I was in control of how I looked and also how I felt. That's why, despite all Kerri's gloomy warnings, I'm not going to go back to the way I was.'

I laughed. 'Kerri wouldn't win any awards for the diplomat of the year.'

'And anyway, you didn't have time to do much with me or anyone else last year, especially after you met Rion.'

I looked at him, feeling puzzled. 'Didn't I? Well, he was staying at our house and all, so it was natural we were together sometimes.'

'Sometimes? More like *all* the time.' Harry gave a small laugh and then added, 'He even came to that barbecue with you, even though he wasn't invited.'

I gave an elaborate shudder. 'Don't remind me of that, please. It wasn't one of my best moments.'

He looked away for a moment. 'Mine either.'

I remembered the kiss Harry had tried to give me. I knew I had to say something so we could put it behind us. 'Harry, I'm really sorry about what happened that day. Believe me, I never meant to hurt you. I like you too much for that. It's just that you took me by surprise.'

Looking back at me, he waved a hand and said, 'Don't worry about it, it's in the past. My timing was never very good, and I think I was kind of jealous of Rion. But I'm over all that now. You don't have to worry. I won't try anything like that again. Let's just stay friends, hey, like we used to be.'

That was exactly what I wanted, too, but hearing Harry say it made me think. Would I really reject him again if he tried to kiss me? The thing was, he really had taken me by surprise at the barbecue because I'd only ever thought of him as a friend. But now I wondered.

Was that the only reason I'd turned my head when he tried to kiss me? And, stupidly, now that he seemed totally over any feelings he might've had for me, there was a perverse little part of me that felt miffed and sad at the same time. But I had to correct one thing I'd heard him say.

'I don't know why you would ever be jealous of Rion,' I said. 'I never thought of him in that way. In fact, he used to get on my nerves sometimes. He was always going on about studying and health food. He just needed a place to stay for a while, and you know my mum, she's always taking in strays. In fact, I think she misses him more than I do.'

Harry looked at me in surprise. 'It seemed like you two were really into each other.'

I shrugged. 'There was never anything between us.'

Harry still seemed unconvinced, but all he said was, 'I guess we've all changed over the summer.'

On the way home that afternoon I thought about what Harry had said. I remembered Rion, all right. After all, he'd stayed with my family for months. It's just that I couldn't remember very much about him other than he'd been nerdy, arrogant and liked to give me long, meaningless lectures full of advice on how I should live my life. I wondered how I'd put up with him for so long.

# Chapter Five

The next day at school, reality set in. The teachers loaded us with so much work and so many assignments that if I did everything they told us to do I'd barely have time for eating and sleeping until Easter. I kept hearing the same thing over and over again. This was year twelve, and if we expected to get into the courses we wanted at uni, or if we even expected to do anything that was worth doing next year, we'd better study.

Blah, blah, blah. Over it already.

Sadly, I realised the summer holidays were well and truly in the past.

Naturally, Kerri was already freaking out. She even brought her physics book to lunch and read it while she was eating her wrap. She totally ignored us.

Lou was late to lunch, but when she came she was saucer eyed and excited. 'Hey, Zoe, did you hear the news?'

'No, what?'

She sat down beside me. 'Rion is back.' She looked at me as though waiting for my reaction.

'What? I don't believe it. I haven't seen him this morning. How do you know?'

'I heard Jas tell Chelsea when I was walking behind them just now.'

I looked over at where Jas and Chelsea were sitting. Jas caught my eye and sent me a glance that was anything but friendly. 'Nah,' I said, 'she's just fooling with you, stirring up trouble as usual.'

Kerri looked up from her book. 'Actually, Lou's right, he was in my physics class this morning.'

'And you never thought to mention it before now?' I said.

She shrugged. 'I forgot.'

I shook my head. That was Kerri all over. Nothing was more important to her than studying. But Jas knowing about it made sense. She took physics as well. I thought about the news. Rion was back and he hadn't even tried to get in touch with our family, despite the fact that he'd stayed with us for months.

Typical. I was annoyed but not overly concerned. The two of us had never got on.

'Didn't he get in touch with you to let you know he was back?' Harry said, echoing my thoughts.

'Why should he?' I shrugged. 'It makes no difference to me. He was always arrogant and caught up in himself.'

'Wow, you sure have changed your opinion about him since last year,' Lou said.

I was getting tired of everyone telling me how much I'd been into Rion. I wasn't. End of story.

'You've got it all wrong, Lou,' I said. 'I'm surprised he's back so soon, that's all.' I bit into my sandwich, wishing someone would change the subject.

Lou, taking the hint said, 'So, Harry, are you going to that play Ms D told us about?'

He shook his head. 'Don't think so.'

'But it's the same play we're studying in class and Ms D said it would really help us in the assignment we're doing on *Macbeth*. What about you, Zoe? You're into English and everything.'

'Shakespeare? Not my thing,' I said.

'Kerri? You want to get a good mark, don't you?' Lou was being unusually persistent.

Kerri lifted her head from the massive book she was reading and gave Lou a look of irritation. 'I am studying here, you know. And no, I'm not going. I've got far too many assignments. I might watch something online.'

I rolled my eyes at Lou and Harry. Then I said, 'How come you're so keen to go, Lou? Didn't know you liked English that much.'

She sighed. 'I don't. Mum's making me go. She thinks it'll be good for me to get some culture.'

A voice cut across us. 'Actually, I've heard the 1979 movie version with Judy Dench and Ian McKellen is quite good. You can probably watch it from home online, and it'll certainly be far better than some amateur production performed locally.'

There was only one voice that could sound like that. I looked up and, sure enough, there was Rion. He looked as good as he always did, with his dark hair drifting over even darker eyes. But I knew the package didn't match the contents. Talk about false advertising.

'Rion, you're back,' I said, stating the obvious.

He smiled at me. 'Hi, Zoe, it's good to see you again.' His eyes were kind of warm and melting, and he seemed friendlier than I remembered. That surprised me.

'I thought your uncle had taken you off to the Amazon jungle or somewhere on one of his photo shoots,' I said.

'My uncle finished his work and decided to bring me back for my senior year.' He looked at the rest of the group. 'Do you mind if I join you guys?'

Everyone was too surprised at the courtesy to say no. He sat down beside me and I moved over to give him plenty of room.

'So where are you living now?' Harry asked Rion. I noticed his tone was icily polite.

'My uncle has a townhouse, actually not too far from where you live, Zoe.'

'Great,' Harry said in an undertone.

'How are your parents?' Rion asked me.

'Good.'

'I'd really like to see them again,' he said.

'You'll have to come by sometime and say hello to them,' I said politely. And then I added, 'I'm sure they'll be surprised to hear you're back, especially since they haven't heard from you for months.' I couldn't help adding that last dig.

He looked embarrassed. 'I'm sorry about that. It was difficult communicating from … the Amazon. But I'd really like to see them. I've missed … you all. Perhaps I can come by this afternoon after school.'

Seriously? I really didn't think he'd want to bother.

'Mum's going to be late. She has one of those parent-teacher interview things, and Dad's going to be late, too.' I didn't want to see Rion today or any other time, really. Even the ton of homework I had to do was more appealing than spending time with him.

'Oh, okay. Some other time then.'

He seemed genuinely disappointed. Another surprise.

I started to feel a bit guilty. Maybe it had been hard communicating from the Amazon or whatever remote area he and his uncle had been in.

'You can come round this weekend, if you want.' At times like this, I hated that I'd inherited my mum's empathy gene.

He brightened up. 'Yes, I will. It'll be great to see your mum and dad again.'

I tried not to sigh too loudly. Might as well get it over with.

'And catch up with you, too,' he added.

I nodded, not really knowing what else to say.

'So,' Lou said in a small voice, 'no one is going to see the play, hey?'

I never realised how persistent she could be, considering she used her words like they were rationed. She really didn't want to go to this play alone. I found myself saying, 'I guess I could go. I'd really like to keep that A in English I got last year.'

Lou beamed at me. 'Great. That's just awesome, Zoe.'

Harry said, 'Maybe I could stand being bored for two hours. I'll go, too.'

Lou looked like all her Christmases had come at once. 'Fantastic, Harry.'

Then Rion said, 'You know, I think it might be really interesting to see how a local production handles Shakespeare. I might come as well.'

He and Harry looked at each other, and I have to say not in an altogether friendly way. I had no idea what was going on there.

'Can you people be quiet? I might as well try to study at McDonald's.' Kerri got up and shut her book. 'I'm going to the library.' No one tried to stop her.

Lou looked round at everybody and clapped her hands. 'Yay,' she said, 'we're going to have such fun.'

I seriously doubted that.

# Chapter Six

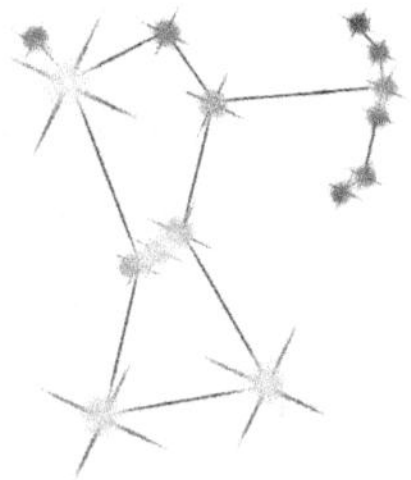

I closed my laptop. Even the episode of *Happy Days* where the Fonz meets Robin Williams as Mork, the alien, hadn't cheered me up. When I'd seen it in the past I'd thought it was funny because Mork from Ork was so different to real aliens but at the same time was so similar. Like Mork, I was still trying to work out how to get girls—well, one in particular. And as for the Fonz, forget it. I had nowhere near his success rate. I wasn't cool like Fonzie or funny like Mork. In fact, it seemed I was very forgettable.

Being back was worse than I'd thought it would be. No one was exactly overjoyed to see me, especially not Zoe. Of course, I knew she wouldn't remember me as an alien, and definitely wouldn't remember her feelings for me, but I'd hoped there would still be some connection. I knew that to have those expectations was stupid, selfish, idiotic—all of that.

Zoe seemed to have reverted to the way she was when we first encountered each other, when all she'd wanted to do was get rid of me. We could have been strangers, the way she talked to me at school. But that was what I wanted, wasn't it? My only consolation was that she had invited me to her house on the weekend, but even then I felt that she was only being polite.

I had to accept it: Zoe didn't really want to see me.

And despite my excellent memory I hardly recognised Harry. He must have had a readjustment in both his diet and his exercise regime. I also noticed that the female students were taking an interest in him, something that hadn't happened previously.

Harry wasn't the only one whose appearance had changed. Zoe looked different, too. Her dark brown hair was longer and had a natural curl. She had lost some of her boyish slenderness and was looking curvier. Last year I told her she looked about twelve. That was no longer the case. She looked more beautiful than ever.

I wasn't the only one who had noticed. Harry was still interested in her, I could tell. I saw the way he looked at her when he thought no one was watching. And as for Zoe being interested in Harry, well, maybe. Why that should upset me I didn't know. After all, I should be happy for her. Harry was kind and would make someone—Zoe—a suitable boyfriend.

I'd even suggested it to her once myself. But that was before he looked the way he did now, back when I knew there wasn't much chance of it happening.

Now it seemed likely; I calculated that there was an 89.632 % chance that they might date.

The laws of chance and probability sucked, as Zoe would say.

I decided to go for a run, and I would *not* run past her house. After all, I was a highly intelligent being with over four thousand years of experience, both worldly and otherworldly. Why would I care what a sixteen-year-old human girl thought of me?

'How lovely to see you, Rion,' Mum said as she gave him a hug.

She just happened to be getting out of her car as he was jogging past our house. And I just happened to be outside putting a bag of rubbish in the bin. And of course he stopped running and came over to talk to us.

Naturally, Mum was surprised, I hadn't had time to tell her, but I was even more surprised by the warmth of her greeting.

'So, when did you get back?' she said.

'We returned a few days ago. My uncle finished his work in Brazil and decided we should come back here for a while so I could finish school.' Rion smiled back at her. 'It's very nice to see you too, Mrs Brennan. I hope you've had a good summer.'

'Not bad, though of course we all missed you, especially Zoe,' Mum said, shooting me a look.

What was Mum talking about? I had so not missed him.

'Why don't you come inside and have a cool drink or something, and tell us all about your adventures? The Amazon, it must have been so exciting. I envy you going to such an exotic and interesting area of the world.'

Rion looked uncertain, but just in case he said yes, I jumped in. 'Mum, he's probably got to get back to his uncle. And besides, it's getting late.'

Luckily, Rion could take a hint. 'Thanks, Mrs Brennan, but Zoe's right, I do have to get back. I just came out for a run.'

'Then you live nearby,' Mum said. 'Of course you do. I remember when you first came to stay with us, you said your uncle had a place in the neighbourhood.'

'Yes, in one of those new townhouses on McCarthy Street.'

'Then you both must come over for dinner on Saturday night. We'd love to catch up with you. And we'll have a chance to get acquainted with your uncle, too.'

'Thanks, but my uncle's not a very sociable kind of person. He wouldn't want to impose,' Rion said. 'And he's usually very busy.'

Thank God, I thought. Rion didn't want a long, boring family dinner any more than I did.

'Nonsense,' my mother said. 'You're like family to us, Rion. Tell your uncle we'll expect you at six o'clock. I really look forward to hearing about those Amazon adventures you two have been on.' My mother spoke in her most bossy schoolteacher's voice. Not many people could argue with her when she spoke like that, not even my dad.

'Then I'll let him know. Thank you.'

'No need to thank me yet, you know what my cooking's like.' She gave a laugh and hugged him again. 'Now, you'd better be off. I don't want you to keep your uncle waiting.'

'Goodbye, Mrs Brennan, Zoe,' he said and then, giving a wave, he turned and jogged back down the street.

'Muuum, did you have to invite them to dinner?' I said as she went back to her car and unloaded the bag of books and test papers that seemed to come home every night. 'Rion doesn't want to come.'

Mum looked at me in surprise. 'Of course he wants to come. He was just being considerate of his uncle. And what's wrong with you, Zoe? I would've thought you'd be delighted to see him again. You've been miserable ever since he left.'

What was Mum talking about? Everyone seemed to think Rion and I were good friends.

We walked into the house, and I went upstairs feeling confused and depressed, a total contrast to the way I'd felt when the day began. I had to put it down to one thing—Rion's return. I hadn't expected it, and for some reason it made me feel really weird.

I mean, I didn't like him, that was a given. But when I met him today, at lunchtime and just now, I'd felt like there was something between us that I was missing. I just didn't know what it was.

To me, he was just this random guy who'd stayed at our place for a few months because he had family issues. My parents were real suckers for things like that, especially my mum. Maybe that's why she seemed to like him so much. She just couldn't help herself. She couldn't resist anyone who needed help. Dad said that was why he'd never take her to a Third World country—they'd come back totally broke. Not because she'd bought anything, but because she'd given all their money away. And he wasn't completely joking.

Yes, that must be it. That's why my mum had greeted Rion so warmly. As for me, I couldn't care less about him. There were far too many other important things to worry about this year. For some reason, the image of Harry Crosby flitted through my mind.

*Forget it.* I didn't want a repeat of last year, where mixed signals between us almost caused me to lose his friendship. Harry was just a friend, a good one, but still just a friend. He wanted that. I wanted that. End of story.

# Chapter Seven

'You did what?' Archimedes didn't look happy.

'It's only dinner,' I said. I wasn't looking forward to it any more than he was, but that was because *he* would be with me. Archimedes was ... unusual. Still, what harm could he do in a couple of hours, I asked myself.

'I cannot believe you accepted a social invitation on my behalf without consulting me. Have you no idea of etiquette at all?' Archimedes threw his hands in the air. 'You do have a rudimentary understanding of basic manners, do you not?'

I felt like saying, 'More than you do,' but I refrained. He was, after all, my superior, which technically meant he could tell me what to do and I would, more or less, have to do it.

'It was hard to say no. If you knew Mrs Brennan, you'd understand.' I really liked Zoe's mum. She was one of the kindest people I knew, especially to me. I'd never realised before that mothers could be so warm.

Not that I was in any way criticising my own birth mother. She gave me everything I required in terms of nutrients, health and education. She had been justifiably proud when I was accepted into the space program because it meant she had done her job of bringing me up correctly. We had a mutually courteous relationship and I had been very respectful of her. It's just that we didn't overly display our emotions. That was our way.

Being organic life forms, I knew that my birth mother and father would have passed away a long time ago. It seemed pointless to miss them after all this time.

But I had missed Zoe's mother. I couldn't explain it.

Archimedes collapsed onto the sofa and raised a hand to his brow. He was rather theatrical at times. It wasn't as if his hosts had included any of the great playwrights, such as Shakespeare, Moliere or Euripides. No, Archimedes loved science and mathematics, which was why he had named himself after the famous Greek mathematician. But I thought he must also have had an actor or two as hosts, because he certainly knew how to play the drama queen.

'Are you all right, Archimedes? You sure you wouldn't like a glass of filtered water?'

'No, I shall rally,' he said, completely missing my sarcasm. 'I am made of sterner stuff than that. I knew that my duty as your guardian would involve unpleasant events. I assume this is just the first of many.' He looked up at me. 'You do realise we shall have to immerse ourselves in information on Brazil, and in particular the Amazon rainforest. I don't know about you, but I've never had a host from that part of the world.'

And then panic set in. I knew Zoe's family would be expecting tall tales and stories about our exploits in the Amazon, and, like Archimedes, I had no knowledge of that area. We needed to study.

'Do find something on Eye Tube or whatever it's called,' he said. 'I have approximately one hour, thirty-six minutes and twenty-two seconds, no, make that twenty-one seconds, before I return to the mothercloud. Perhaps I will have that glass of water. I feel quite faint.'

He wasn't the only one. Ignoring his request, I opened my laptop and began to search.

Saturday was a big day, no exaggeration. Mum was going way over the top with this dinner thing. I helped Dad tidy up the garden, and even cleaned the bathroom, my least favourite job in the world.

Mum had decided to do something fancy. She was going to make beef Wellington or, if you wanted to be very *Master Chef*-y about it, *filet de bœuf en croûte*. Basically, it was an expensive piece of beef wrapped up in pastry and roasted in the oven. I knew it was way beyond my mother's expertise. Both Dad and I tried to convince her that a barbecue might be easier, or even a Coles cooked chook. But she would not be moved. She could be very stubborn at times.

'Dad,' I said, as we were collecting the grass trimmings and putting them on the garden beds for mulch, 'do you think it might be an idea to have something in reserve, just in case, you know, things don't go according to plan?'

He looked at me and winked. 'You and I, possum, are on the same wavelength. What about I get a barbecued chicken and a couple of salads and put them in the fridge in the garage. Your mum doesn't even have to know they're there. But in case something goes wrong, and I'm not saying it will, we'll be prepared.'

I breathed a sigh of relief. No matter what happened with Mum's cooking, the night wouldn't be a complete disaster. Though in other ways it might totally suck.

Dad wasn't looking forward to it either, because although he really liked Rion, he said the uncle had seemed a bit of a 'tosser' when he met him the day

Archimedes came to our house to take Rion off on his trip to the Amazon.

I hadn't met Rion's uncle, but I imagined that if he was anything like his nephew, that was probably an accurate description.

I avoided the kitchen because I didn't want to look at the disaster scene I was sure I'd find there. I could hear the sounds of pots and pans being banged, alternating with Mum singing. She only sang when she was super-stressed, so that wasn't a good sign. I crept upstairs to the strains of 'Dancing Queen' emerging from the kitchen. She usually turned to ABBA when she wanted to psych herself up.

*Sigh*. I wondered how long a night could last.

After showering and straightening my hair, I faced the eternal problem of what to wear. This wasn't a date or anything, but I didn't want to look like a slob, either. Not that I was out to impress anyone.

I slipped on my black jeans and a white blouse. Perfect if I was a waiter. I ditched the top for a striped T-shirt and looked in the mirror. Ha! Yes, the prison look was very in this year. Sigh again. Six changes later, I went back to the skinny black jeans and added a sleeveless pink top. Dangly earrings completed the look.

I didn't know why I bothered. It wasn't even as if Rion would notice unless I had a T-shirt printed with the periodic table from chemistry. I knew he would think that was ultra-cool.

At five-thirty, I ventured downstairs to see what havoc Mum had managed to create. The dining-room table held a vase of flowers from the garden and some long, tapered candles. What? Was the royal family coming or something?

I peeked in the kitchen and saw the vegetables gently steaming on the stovetop, the gravy simmering in a pan, and there was a nice smell wafting out of the oven. Everything looked serene and organised, like a picture from the *Women's Weekly*.

Someone came up behind me. 'Snooping, eh?'

I jumped and turned around. 'Mum, don't scare me like that.'

She skirted around me and went to the stove to check the gravy. 'Yes, just right, I'll turn it off now and reheat when we're ready to serve.'

'Things are looking pretty good in here,' I said, trying not to sound too surprised.

'Yes, they are, aren't they?' Mum gave me a smug smile. 'Good, I'm glad to see you're dressed. I'm going up to get changed. Keep an eye open for when our guests arrive.'

A little while later she came back downstairs in one of her summery, sleeveless dresses, her blonde hair down for a change.

'Hey, you look nice, Mum.'

She smiled at me. 'Thanks, darling, so do you. We scrub up well, don't we?'

She had to say that, she was my mum. But my dark, unmanageable hair came from my dad, which was okay for him because he kept it so short. I would have preferred to have Mum's sleek blonde hair. The universe was so unfair at times.

There was a knock at the door. I whipped out my phone to check the time. It was precisely six o'clock. Yep, I'd figured that would be the case.

Rion's uncle actually looked okay for someone who was ancient—well, forty-five or fifty, at least. He was dressed a bit formally, in a blue shirt, long trousers and lace-ups. (Dad was in shorts, T-shirt and sandals.) Like Rion, his uncle looked like he worked out, but the resemblance ended there. His sandy hair and blue eyes were a complete contrast to Rion, who had those dark, brooding kind of looks—very Damon from *The Vampire Diaries*.

After the somewhat awkward introductions were made, during which Rion's uncle actually kissed my mother's hand (who does *that*?), we sat down in the lounge.

Archimedes took one of the comfortable armchairs, Dad took the other one, and Mum, Rion and I crowded together on the sofa. At this stage I was so wishing we'd had a barbecue and were sitting outside, but Mum had said there were too many mosquitoes.

Archimedes (he insisted we all call him that, even me) looked around and said, 'What a charming little house you have, and so suitably decorated for people of your station in life.' He gave us a beaming smile.

I could feel Rion cringe beside me.

Dad cleared his throat and asked if anyone would like a drink.

'Refreshments, what an excellent idea,' Archimedes said. 'I usually stick to filtered water, but since this is a special occasion I will have a glass of the 2005 Vieux Château Certan. As Bordeaux goes, it's rather smooth on the palate, I believe.'

I had to bite my lips to keep from laughing. Obviously photojournalists earned a lot more than my parents.

Dad said, 'I don't actually have that one in my wine cellar.' Mum gave him a look, so he added, 'But I do have a nice Brown Brothers Shiraz you might like to try.'

'Whatever is convenient, my dear man, and if I don't like it, I just won't drink it.'

Dad left the room quickly and Archimedes settled back in his chair. 'Would someone put the air-conditioning on in here?' he said. 'It is rather warm. I need a temperature-controlled environment. Twenty-three degrees would be perfect.'

Mum flicked the control and said, 'I'll just pop into the kitchen to see how dinner's going.'

'Of course, dear lady, do whatever is necessary. I shall be perfectly fine here with these young people.'

Great. It had been Mum's idea to have this dinner, and now both she and Dad had bailed on me. But to my relief, Archimedes didn't feel it was necessary to make any more attempts at conversation. He leaned back on the headrest and closed his eyes, completely ignoring us.

Rion looked at me and mouthed silently, *I'm sorry.*

I shrugged and said quietly, 'It's okay.'

We sat in embarrassed silence for a few minutes.

Finally he said, 'So, how have you been, Zoe?'

'Good, fine, what about you? How have things been the last few months?'

'I've been busy, you know, learning Mandarin Chinese and playing online chess.'

I looked at him in surprise. 'In the middle of the Amazon jungle?'

He looked flustered for a moment, and then said, 'Yes, at night. When we weren't trekking down the Amazon, of course.'

I looked over at his uncle, who appeared to be sleeping. Somehow I couldn't imagine Archimedes roughing it in the jungle. And his pale skin didn't look like it had seen much sun.

Dad came bustling in with a tray of drinks, which was just as well as the conversation between Rion and me was going nowhere fast. I took another sneak peak at the clock on the wall. Six twenty-five, one minute later than the last time I'd checked. Were the hands stuck or something?

Archimedes was snoring lightly in his chair when Dad put the glass of wine beside him.

Rion said, rather loudly, 'Uncle Archimedes.'

Archimedes spluttered, snorted and opened his eyes, looking around. 'What? Oh yes, I must have fallen asleep for a moment. I do find this physical body such a nuisance, it's so tiring to be organic at times.'

'He's got jet lag. It's a long way from South America,' Rion said, sounding just a little desperate.

Archimedes looked puzzled. 'South America?'

'Yes, where we've just travelled from,' Rion said. Then he added, 'Where you've been on assignment as a photojournalist.'

'No need to shout, my hearing is perfect.'

Dad and I exchanged glances, and I could see he was trying not to laugh. Instead, he said, 'How's the wine, Archimedes?'

Archimedes took up his glass and sipped. Then he took a second sip, and a third. 'Actually, it's not bad. Not half as vinegary as I thought it would be.'

Luckily, at that point Mum came in and said in a sing-song-y voice, 'Dinner's ready, everyone.'

There are times when my mother surprises me. Tonight was one of them. How she managed to cook such a perfectly amazing dinner was beyond me. The pastry wrapped around the meat was buttery and flaky. The beef inside wasn't overdone, but pink in the middle the way it should be. The gravy wasn't lumpy or too salty or any of the other things that Mum usually did to gravy. In fact, it was perfect. Even the vegetables weren't overcooked.

Archimedes must have enjoyed it, because he had three helpings.

'Ah, *filet de bœuf en croûte*, a classic dish, my dear, and you've done it proud. My compliments to the chef,' he said, and waved an airy hand.

Mum beamed. It wasn't often she received praise for her cooking. 'But you must tell me about your adventures in the Amazon. I've been dying to hear about them.'

Archimedes put down his napkin. 'Ah, yes, the Amazon. What wonderful times we had, didn't we?' He looked over at Rion.

Rion sat up straight, like he used to do in class when he answered a teacher's question. 'Yes, it's a fascinating place. Did you know, for instance, that it contains over half of the planet's rainforests and has an estimated 390 billion trees, of which there are 16,000 species.'

Mum nodded. 'That is amazing.'

'And,' he continued, 'it covers over seven million square kilometres, most of which is in Brazil, though it also covers smaller areas of Peru, Columbia, Venezuela, Ecuador, Bolivia, Guyana, Suriname and French Guiana.' He looked around the table and smiled at us.

'You always did have a good head for facts, Rion,' Dad said. 'No wonder you do so well in school. But what did you see actually?'

'I think that's one for you, Uncle Archimedes. You are, after all, the photographer.'

Archimedes took a sip of wine and put his glass down. 'As you know, wet, tropical forests are species-rich biomes. In the Amazon there are some 40,000 plant species, 2200 types of fish, 1294 types of birds, 428 types of amphibians, 378 types of reptiles and, oh yes, 427 species of mammals. I must say, this is a surprisingly drinkable wine.' He reached out for the bottle and filled his glass again.

Obviously Archimedes was as good at facts as his nephew. But there was something I really wanted to know. 'Did you see any anacondas?'

'Anacondas? Oh yes, an incredible number.' Archimedes waved the hand that held his wine glass and a drop of wine spilt on the tablecloth.

'Really? Have you got any photos to show us on your phone?' That, I thought, would be cool.

'Phone?' he looked confused.

'Uncle Archimedes forgot his phone tonight,' Rion said.

'What about you, though? You must have some pictures,' I said to Rion.

He shook his head.

I looked at him, my suspicions increasing. And then I remembered from before that Rion didn't have a phone.

'Would anybody like coffee and desert?' Mum said. 'I didn't make it, but there's some mango cheesecake.'

'My dear lady, you are bounty itself,' Archimedes said. 'Such a wonderful hostess, and such a fine specimen of human female beauty.' He leaned towards her with a glassy stare and a smile that was a bit wobbly. 'I raise my glass to you.' Lifting it to his lips, he finished his wine and plonked the glass back on the table. He gave a small burp.

Mum didn't quite know where to look, but, being a schoolteacher, she was used to handling difficult students. 'It's so kind of you,' she said. 'Why don't you move into the lounge and make yourself comfortable, and I'll bring out the coffee.'

She expertly whipped away his plate and wine glass and nodded to me, saying, 'Zoe, help clear the table, won't you?' She looked meaningfully at the nearly empty second bottle of wine. The first one was long finished. And he was the only one drinking because Dad had had a beer and Mum was drinking water.

But before I could say anything, Rion got up and grabbed the wine bottle along with the potato bowl. 'I'll help.'

Dad helped Archimedes up from the table since it was obvious he wouldn't make it on his own.

'Oh, thank you, my dear man. How kind of you. I shall be glad to shed this mortal coil. I'm feeling slightly unwell.'

Dad said nothing, and I guessed it was because he didn't want to say the wrong thing—unlike Archimedes, who didn't seem to worry about that kind of thing at all. He was beyond weird. I was starting to feel just a little bit sorry for Rion.

Mum, Rion and I had the table cleared in no time. I think we were all hoping to get this evening over with as quickly as possible.

'My uncle is suffering badly from jet lag,' Rion said, when we were in the kitchen. 'He's not quite himself tonight.'

Mum laughed and patted his shoulder. 'Don't worry about it, Rion. I don't think I've ever received so many compliments about my cooking in my life.'

'It was an excellent dinner, Mrs Brennan. I always thought you were a good cook.'

That last statement was probably one of the biggest lies Rion had ever told in his life. But it was sweet of him. He wasn't quite as bad as I remembered. And he was a big help in the kitchen.

The three of us worked like a well-oiled machine, and in no time at all we'd whisked the coffees and desert into the lounge, where Archimedes had fallen asleep again. Dad was reading the paper.

Rion woke up his uncle, who shook himself and looked at his watch. 'Oh dear, look at the time. It's nearly nine o'clock. I really must leave immediately.'

'But you haven't had your coffee or dessert yet,' Mum said.

'No time, no time,' he said, struggling up out of his chair.

Rion, who was starting to look a bit panicky, helped him up. 'I think I'd better get my uncle home,' he said, looking apologetic.

'Of course,' Dad said. 'Let me walk you to the car. Is your uncle …'

'No, he's not driving. We walked here.'

'I can give you a lift home, if you like,' Dad said.

'Thanks, Mr Brennan, but there's really no need. It's not far and the fresh air will do us both good.' Rion led a slightly confused Archimedes to the front door.

Archimedes turned just before Rion opened the door and said, 'Thank you for a most enjoyable evening. The food was splendid, the wine was quite drinkable and the company was surprisingly adequate. You thave acquitted yourselves well tonight. Especially you, dear lady.' He beamed at my mother. 'You outshone them all with your magnificence and your beauty.'

I watched him, fascinated, as he leaned towards her. Surely he wasn't going to kiss Mum. Rion pulled him away in the nick of time and opened the front door, pushing him out of it.

'Thank you so much, Mr and Mrs Brennan, for a lovely evening. See you later, Zoe.' He hurried out after his uncle and quickly closed the door behind him.

And I'd thought this evening was going to be boring. Just shows you how wrong you can be.

# Chapter Eight

When the door closed, Mum, Dad and I all looked at each other and burst out laughing. We couldn't help ourselves; it had been building up all night.

Finally Mum stopped and said, 'Shhh, he might hear us.'

'I doubt if he'd hear a freight train go by at the moment,' Dad said.

'I thought he was going to kiss you, Mum.'

'If Rion hadn't hauled his uncle back so quickly, I might've been tempted to lay hands on him myself,' Dad said, not looking quite so amused.

'Oh, don't be silly, he was just a little tipsy.'

'A little?' Dad said. 'For someone who has such expensive tastes in wine, he didn't mind polishing off nearly two bottles of my twelve-dollar plonk.'

Mum went into the lounge room and collapsed on the sofa. 'I hope there's some left. I was so worried I'd spoil the dinner that I never had a sip to drink. But I could use one now, I'm beat.'

'I'll get you a glass, and don't worry about the dishes. Zoe and I will do them.' Dad headed towards the kitchen.

'No need.' Mum lifted her feet onto the coffee table. 'Rion helped Zoe and me clear up, and he also stacked the dishwasher.'

'Nice of him,' Dad said. 'He certainly isn't anything like his uncle. I'll be back with your wine in a moment.' The kitchen door swung closed behind him.

'You did good tonight, Mum,' I said, sitting beside her and putting my head on her shoulder.

'Thank you, my dear lady, I rather believe I did.'

We both burst into giggles again.

'I really shouldn't make fun of Rion's uncle,' Mum said. 'I'm sure he means well. But he has such an odd way of expressing himself. I mean, he really didn't tell us anything about their Amazon trip except for facts and figures.'

'I know, right? And neither did Rion.' I sat up and looked at her. 'You might even think they didn't go there.'

'Of course they did. I just think that Rion was too embarrassed by his uncle's behaviour to say much, and his uncle probably thought he was doing a fine job by giving us all that information.'

Dad came in with the wine for Mum and a beer for himself. 'He's just an old windbag,' he said, passing Mum the glass.

'Not so old,' Mum said with a smile.

'Says the lady whose magnificence and beauty outshone us all,' Dad said.

Mum just shook her head at him and laughed.

I got up. 'I'm going to bed. I think I've had enough excitement for one night.'

When I reached my bed, I flopped down onto it. It had been a long day and a strange night. Who would've imagined Rion with such an unusual uncle? But as for Rion himself, though he wasn't chatty, he wasn't as bad as I remembered. Maybe I'd judged him too harshly.

I was just thinking about getting into my pyjamas when I heard the ping of a text on my phone.

*Sorry about my uncle. He doesn't usually drink. Will your parents ever speak to me again? Or you?*

I looked at the text. Rion obviously was embarrassed, not that I could blame him. But it wasn't his fault that his uncle was so weird. I was surprised to see a text from him. I'd assumed he didn't have a phone, because he didn't have one last year. That had been one of the many strange things about him.

*You have a phone?*

*Yes, but only recently. Lou gave me your number. Is it OK to text you?*

*Sure. Don't worry about tonight. My parents will never think badly of you.*

I stopped. For some reason, that was true. They really liked Rion, which made me wonder why I didn't. Well, strictly speaking that wasn't true. I didn't actually *dislike* him. In fact, at the moment I wasn't sure how I felt about him.

His text came back quickly. *And you?*

I wanted to keep it light. *We're cool. Too bad you missed out on cheesecake. See you Monday.*

It was only a few seconds before the next text came pinging back.

*Sorry to have missed that—despite its high calorie and fat content.*

And that's precisely what I meant by strange. Who says that? I was about to put my phone away when another text came.

*You looked very nice tonight. I like your hair. Now that it's longer, it balances your round face.*

Was that supposed to be a compliment? I struggled for a reply.

*Thanks, Rion. You looked nice, too. I'll bring you some cheesecake on Monday.* You looked nice too? How lame was that. Backspace, backspace, backspace. *Thanks, Rion.*

Before I could change my mind I pressed send. Oops. I'd left in the bit about the cheesecake. Whatever.

I got into my pyjamas and snuggled into bed, yawning. And then my phone pinged again.

*Thanks, Zoe. We can share that cheesecake on Monday.*

That wasn't what I meant at all. I would bring him a small piece in a Tupperware dish and that was that. I didn't want us to share it like we were a couple or something. How could guys get it so wrong sometimes?

I gave up. Crazy didn't even begin to describe the day this had been.

If Archimedes hadn't dematerialised so quickly when we left Zoe's house, I would have sent him into outer space myself. How could he have behaved so badly? He was nearly five thousand years old.

I knew he'd never actually had alcohol before, though he tried to pretend he knew everything about it. I blamed the French aristocrat he'd inhabited during the French Revolution for his so-called 'taste'. Also, the London banker with the excellent wine cellar, Archimedes' last host, had to bear some of the blame. But the biggest culprit tonight was Archimedes himself. He had made a complete and utter fool of himself, and me, too. He just didn't get how to act as a human.

I was stretched out on my bed, staring into the darkness, my phone beside me. How could I ever make it up to Zoe and her parents? She'd been kind when I texted her to apologise. She was even going to bring me some cheesecake on Monday. But she was still treating me like a stranger.

Seeing how Archimedes had acted made me realise I hadn't been so different from him in the beginning. I'd also been arrogant and not always very diplomatic. But I'd learnt a lot since then. I'd even complimented Zoe on her appearance, though I wasn't sure I'd got it quite right. I was still on a learning curve.

But I'd learnt something even more important over the past few months on my own. I had learnt about feelings. I'd discovered that they weren't as unnecessary or unwise as I'd originally thought. And I knew I had them for Zoe. I wondered if she would ever have them for me.

School was the last place I wanted to be on Monday. I wasn't sure about the Rion thing, whether to bring him cheesecake or not. I didn't want him to get the wrong impression and think I was interested in him. That wouldn't be fair, as I had learnt last year with Harry.

Also, I hadn't done my chemistry homework because it was really hard and I just didn't get it. Maybe Kerri would let me copy her answers. Last year I would have asked Harry, but he wasn't doing chemistry this year.

And also, Mum's hair straightener had died, so my hair was in its natural state of a curly mess. I really needed a decent hair straightener and the money to buy it. Babysitting jobs had been few and far between lately, and I was down on cash.

In English class, Ms D enthusiastically reminded us of the play we had the 'great opportunity' to see.

'Tickets for students are half price,' she said, 'which is such good value for a production at QPAC. And if we can get at least ten students, the school will hire a minibus and subsidise the cost. So, how many of you are thinking of going?' She gazed around the class hopefully.

Lou put her hand up right away, so then I had to. Harry and Rion followed. Everyone else's hands remained firmly down.

'Four? Well, we only need six more. Remember, this is a unique opportunity to see a live production of Shakespeare and we're so fortunate that it's *Macbeth*, the very play we're studying this year. It will help you understand and appreciate this great work. And, undoubtedly, it will help you when you come to do your assignment later in the term, which—if I need to remind you—is worth fifty percent of your first semester's grade.'

I had to admit that Ms D was selling it hard, but her audience was unreceptive. She tried again.

'I know Brisbane Girls' Grammar is sending their entire senior class to the production. I'm sure East Valley High also has just as keen an interest in culture as academic studies.'

Dream on, Ms D, I thought.

Then a hand went up. Ms D pounced on it like a hungry cat on a mouse.

'Yes, Jas, you want to go, too?'

'I was just thinking. If we have to give up our time to go to this, shouldn't it count something towards our final grade? I mean, it is out of school time and it will probably use up at least three or four hours, including travelling time and everything. And, because we're going to have a late night on Thursday, we'll be tired the next day.'

Ms D looked uncertain. 'I can't actually give you credit or marks for going to the performance, Jas. But maybe I could talk to Principal Blewer about letting you have a late start the next day. Would that make a difference to any of you?'

'Does that mean we wouldn't have to go to school on Friday if we went to the play?' Jas asked.

'No, not the whole day, of course,' she said, 'but maybe a couple of hours in the morning. That would be good, wouldn't it?'

'I've heard Grammar is giving their students the next day off so they can rest and also reflect on the play,' Jas said, twirling her hair with one hand.

If I knew anything about Jas, she just made that up on the spot.

'I mean, I'm not used to having a late night during the week. It will really wreck my sleep patterns, and I probably won't be able to concentrate much the next day.'

What a lie that was. When I used to hang out with Jas, she rarely went to bed before midnight, weeknight or not.

'Is that right?' I could see Ms D's defences being worn down. 'I'll have a word with the principal and get back to you.'

'It's just that I'd really love to go, but I don't want to jeopardise my studies by being tired the next day. Teachers often give us pop quizzes on a Friday. And you know the teachers in science and maths wouldn't really be that bothered if students were tired because of an English excursion.'

That was a masterstroke. There was, I'd noticed, always a bit of rivalry between the English teachers and those who taught science and maths.

Ms D bristled. 'I will definitely look into a rest day for the students who attend the performance. We certainly don't want our English students disadvantaged in any way.'

'Thank you, Ms Dawson, that is so nice of you,' Jas said in her sweetest voice, and sat down.

The rest of the class looked at her with admiration. A long weekend just for attending some dumb play.

When Ms D asked again who would be interested in going to see *Macbeth*, just about everyone in the class put up their hands, even Kerri. What chance did anyone have against Jas?

It was a pity I didn't have such powers of persuasion. After our English class, I asked Kerri if I could copy her chemistry homework answers and she looked at me as if I had two heads.

'Why didn't you do your homework?' she said.

Sometimes I wondered if Kerri lived in the real world. There were so many answers to that question. But I could truthfully say, 'I tried, but I didn't quite get it.'

'Then you need to ask Mr Sully. He'll explain it to you.'

'Maybe,' I said, 'but he always makes me feel kind of dumb, and I don't always understand him. Come on, Kerri, it's not going to hurt you. I thought you were my friend. You're supposed to help friends.' Sometimes you had to spell out to Kerri what the normal thing was to do because she didn't always get it.

She shook her red hair. 'It wouldn't be helping you, except to cheat. I'm sorry, Zoe, but you'll never learn that way. And, remember, this is our senior year. We're supposed to take our studies seriously.'

'Okay, you don't have to give me the answers, but maybe you could explain it to me at lunchtime.'

'I haven't got the time. I have to study for my physics test.'

I looked at her in exasperation. She could get an A in physics with her eyes closed, and anyway, she didn't have physics until tomorrow.

'I do take my studies seriously. But I also take my friendships seriously, which you obviously don't.' I turned on my heel and left her standing there.

And promptly bumped into Rion. Smack dab into his rock-hard chest. The Tupperware container holding a piece of cheesecake had been on top of the books I was carrying. I kept hold of the books, but the container went flying and crashed onto the floor.

One of his arms circled around to steady me. 'Whoa, you okay?'

'Yeah, I'm fine. But your cheesecake, not so much.' I looked down to the container, which had come open, spilling its beautiful golden slice of cheesecake on the floor. I moved away from him, but in that microsecond, when he'd had his arm around me, it had felt kind of nice.

'You brought it for me,' he said, and gave me a big smile.

'Ruined now, I'm afraid.'

'That's okay. It's the thought that counts.' He bent down to help me pick it up.

Scraping it off the floor, he popped it into the container. I passed him a clean tissue from my pocket. He wiped his hands first and then the floor. He's come a long way, I thought. Once he would have gone on and on about germs and how he needed to disinfect his hands. Now, why had *that* thought popped into my head?

As we stood up again, he said, 'Did I hear you say something about chemistry to Kerri just then?'

'Yeah, that homework, it was so tough. I really didn't get it.'

'You know, I'm not bad at chemistry.'

That was an understatement if ever there was. Even Kerri McNerd wasn't as smart as he was. 'So I've heard,' I said.

'I could help you, if you like, at lunchtime. We don't have chemistry until last period.'

'That would be awesome,' I said. And it would. For some reason, chemistry was the one subject I couldn't get my head around. But I had to do a couple of science subjects so I could have a choice of courses at uni next year. I still hadn't decided what to do yet.

'Great. We can have lunch together and I'll help you then.'

'Sure, it's a date,' I said and then, when I saw him break out in a huge grin, I thought, oops, wrong choice of words.

At lunchtime, instead of sitting with Harry and the others, we sat under one of the big old fig trees in the corner of the eating area. I was still pretty cranky with Kerri, so I didn't mind not being with her. I just hopped Harry wouldn't think I was snubbing him, which I absolutely wasn't.

'So let's have a look at this homework, then,' Rion said, as he sat down next to me.

We spent the next ten minutes going over the homework. He was actually good at explaining things, and it felt strangely familiar to have him there.

'You've helped me before, haven't you?' I said, looking up into his dark eyes.

'Yeah, a couple of times,' he said, and shook the fringe from his eyes.

That, too, seemed like something I'd seen before. Well, of course I had. He had lived with us, for goodness' sake. Why had I forgotten so much?

'You're not a bad teacher. I think I kind of get it now,' I said.

'You picked it up really quickly.'

We looked at each other and smiled. And I felt something. I'm not sure what, but something. Why did I think I hated him?

We closed our books and took out lunch. I leaned against the bark of the tree trunk and looked up into the leafy greenness, thinking it was kind of nice and that it also felt very familiar.

'Zoe, I was wondering … since we've missed dessert, perhaps we could go for coffee and cake at the shopping centre after school. My treat, of course.' He looked at me all serious like.

It was one thing to study and have lunch together, but this was something else. I was still trying to decide if I liked Rion or not. And I just meant as a friend. Nothing else. It was time to set the record straight.

'Thanks, Rion, but I should go home and study, you know, homework and everything. This is senior year and we do have a lot on.' I couldn't believe the words coming out of my mouth. I hardly convinced myself, so I couldn't hope to convince Rion. But maybe he would get the hint.

He did. He just nodded. 'Sure, I understand. Well, I'd better go. I got my old job back helping to clean up the lab this year.' He grabbed his books and stood up.

'Okay, well, thanks for the help and everything,' I said.

He nodded and headed off in the direction of the science lab.

I was doing him a favour, right? He might as well know I had no interest in him whatsoever. What had made him think I might? I wished I could remember last year better. It seemed such a long time ago, and my memories of Rion were so hazy.

After school, I was just walking out the gate when Harry caught up with me.

'Hey,' he said, 'we missed you at lunch today. I didn't think it'd be long before you and Rion got together again.'

I looked at him, completely puzzled. 'I don't know what you mean. He was just helping me with my chemistry homework because Kerri wouldn't. I'm not too happy with her at the moment.'

'You know what she's like. I would've helped you—I did last year—but I'm not doing chemistry this year.'

'Yeah, I know you would've. But as for Rion and me, there's nothing going on at all. Zilch.'

'That's what you said last year, but you sure spent a lot of time together.'

'I guess that was because we lived in the same house,' I said, wishing Harry would drop it.

'Okay, so if I was to ask you out, you know, just hypothetically, would Rion have to come as well, like he did last year?' Harry looked at me seriously.

I wanted to laugh and make an offhand comment, but I found I couldn't. 'I thought you said we were just going to be friends.' I didn't know why I was suddenly feeling all breathy. This was *Harry*, for goodness' sake.

'Yeah, sure, but friends can do things together, can't they?' His mouth twisted up in a sort of smile.

'You know the only reason Rion went to that barbecue was because Mum and Dad wanted him to make friends. I didn't want him there, that's for sure.'

'You haven't answered my question, Zoe. Will you go out with me? That new Stars Wars movie is out.'

Everyone was streaming past us toward the buses or cars, or to walk home. Could I go out with Harry on a date, a friendship date? After all, I did like sci-fi, and Harry and I used to hang out all the time before we went to high school. It wouldn't be much different to reading comics together when we were ten, would it?

'I guess. What about Lou and Keri?'

Harry shrugged. 'Good luck with trying to pry Keri from her books, and Lou said she was going away this weekend with her folks.'

Without hurting his feelings—and, after last year, I didn't want to chance that again—I had no choice about my answer. 'Sure, why not.' I tried to quell that fluttery feeling inside me.

'You know, it's really hot today,' he said, 'I could do with a cold drink at Macca's. Want to come? We could check out the times of the movie on Saturday. And maybe have a look at the reviews on Rotten Tomatoes.'

'Yeah, okay, but no looking at reviews. They're sure to have spoilers.'

When we got to Macca's, we sat down in the corner with our Cokes.

I looked across the table at Harry, now trim, muscled and looking so different from last year. 'You must've worked so hard over the summer, Harry.'

He nodded. 'At first it wasn't easy, but Uncle Adrian was really supportive. I couldn't have done it without him. And once the weight started to be replaced by muscle it got much easier. It helped that I had a growth spurt, too. Even now, Uncle Adrian keeps in touch and checks on me. I go to the local gym, too.'

'Good on you.'

'You know, you were partly responsible, too,' he said, giving me a shy smile.

'What do you mean?'

'I really liked you last year, but I knew I wasn't good enough for you. I mean, look at you. You're so beautiful and everything. You could have any guy you wanted.'

'That's not true.' I was thinking of my efforts to attract Chad Everett, which had failed spectacularly once he'd seen Jas. 'But thanks anyway. And you shouldn't put yourself down so much. I always liked you, Harry. We've been friends for zonks.'

'Sure, but nothing more, I get it. And that's cool. But would you even be here right now or agreeing to go to the movies with me if I didn't look like I do now?'

That hit me right between the eyes. Was that true? I hoped not. But Harry had changed in more ways than one.

'You're different on the inside, too. You're more confident. Last year you found it hard even to ask me to that family barbecue, even though we've been friends for, like, forever.'

He laughed. 'That was different, because, well, we weren't kids anymore and it was supposed to be a date. We'd never been on a date before. But you're right about one thing. I do feel different. I don't care anymore about what most people think. I've worked too hard to get to this point and if people still don't like me, too bad. But there's one exception. I do care about what you think, Zoe.'

'Hi, Zoe.'

A voice cut across my thoughts. I looked up and there was Rion, with a coffee in his hands.

'And Harry,' he added with a slight lift of his eyebrow.

Oops, awkward. I felt the colour flood my cheeks as I remembered I'd told Rion I couldn't go out with him this afternoon because I had to study. I'd completely forgotten that when I agreed to come here with Harry.

'Oh, hey, Rion,' I said, 'just popped in for a Coke. So hot today, isn't it? I'm on my way home now to do all that studying. Phew, I'll be up for ages.' Could I have sounded any more fake?

'Sure. Well, I'll be seeing you.'

He turned and left quickly, but not so quickly that I didn't see the hurt look in his eyes. I felt like a jerk.

# Chapter Nine

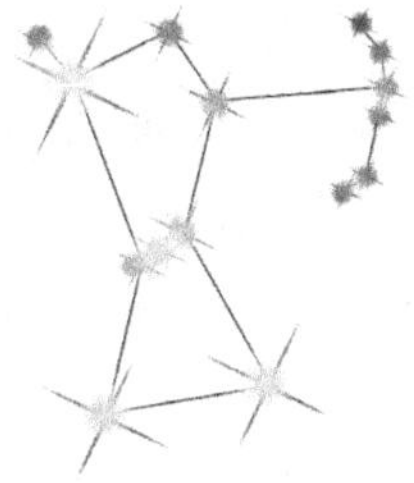

There are times when being human is overrated, and as for feelings of any kind, bad idea. Right now, I would rather have been a bodiless but intelligent being who shared an existence with another host. I could have been with a scientist, or a rock star or even a politician. Life would not have revolved around whether some sixteen-year-old girl liked me or not.

When I reached home, I was in no mood to see Archimedes reclining on the leather sofa with an icepack on his head. It was the first time I'd seen him since Saturday night.

'Oh,' I said, 'you're back.'

'Yes, I thought I'd better pop back to see how you were going. I've had such an awful time of it since Saturday night. Even when I shed this tiresome body, I was really not myself. I might have been a mere stripling of a thousand or so years I was so confused and disoriented. And now I've materialised again, I have such a headache you would not believe it.'

He turned his head to look at the books I'd just put on the kitchen table. 'I do hope you have a more suitable place for those books than the table you're going to eat on.'

I've never before felt the irrational urge to throw an object at anyone, but I resisted the temptation. 'What were you thinking of on Saturday night,' I said, 'drinking so much alcohol and eating so much food? Not to mention embarrassing us both with your inappropriate behaviour.'

'Me? You must be joking. Why, that family positively forced alcohol and food on me. It's a wonder any of these humans live past their teens with their excessive behaviour. Oh, my poor head,' he said, pressing the icepack harder to his forehead.

'No one forced anything on you. And didn't you notice that no one else ate or drank half as much as you did?' I sat down at the table, wanting to stay as far away from him as I could. 'Some guardian you turned out to be.'

He sat up and looked at me. 'Why, I am extremely intelligent and highly skilled. You could not have hoped to find anyone better. After all, you have the benefit of five thousand years of experience and wisdom.'

'I didn't see much of that wisdom on Saturday night,' I said.

Archimedes forgot his icepack for a moment. 'I admit that, never having tasted food or drunk alcohol ever before, it took me by surprise. It was so … enjoyable. I'm not used to living a life that revolves around the senses. I may have dropped my guard a little in my enthusiasm to blend in with the humans. But, other than that, I acquitted myself quite well. I was highly complimentary of their efforts to entertain me. I'm sure they think I'm quite charming. I mean, there really is nothing to this being human, is there? I'm succeeding very well, I have to say, though it's not what I would choose. But sacrifices have to be made for the greater good. I hope you realise that. You ought to be grateful to me.'

'You fell asleep several times, insulted them more than you can imagine, and embarrassed Mrs Brennan. They'll never ask you to dinner again.' I was beginning to feel I'd be better off without a guardian if Archimedes was the best my people could come up with.

'Nonsense. I only had a couple of powernaps to refresh myself, and I never consciously insulted anyone. As for Zoe's mother, she was charmed by my attention. And who would not be? I have to say, she is a lovely specimen of female beauty. She rather reminds me of the Countess

Anna of Hanover. One of my hosts was very smitten with her, but she had many suitors of far greater means so he didn't stand a chance. Pity. I found her rather amusing.'

'Archimedes.'

'Yes?'

'I think you'd better dematerialise. I don't need you at the moment and you're only going to feel the effects of a hangover if you stay in this human body. You may as well return to the mothercloud and rest for a while, a long while. I'll be in touch if I need you.'

'That is thoughtful of you. Some of my good influence must be transmitting itself to you. That is an excellent idea. I must conserve myself, you know. That way I'll be at my peak when you next require my services as guardian.' He stood up and dropped the icepack on the sofa. He gave a theatrical flourish with his hands and slowly dissolved before my eyes.

I breathed a sigh of relief when he was gone. Except that it gave me time to think again, and none of my thoughts were positive.

It was obvious that Harry and Zoe had a thing going, and it wasn't just on Harry's side. I knew it, even if Zoe didn't—yet.

I found myself wishing I hadn't let Archimedes take away Zoe's memories, but then part of me wondered if it would have made any difference. She either liked me or she didn't. And it was pretty obvious she didn't, or at least not as much as Harry Crosby.

I couldn't escape my past. Despite my human body, I knew that inside, in my core, I was still an alien. And maybe that was what Zoe, even though she didn't know it anymore, was turning from—the alien within me. It was a sad and sobering thought. Perhaps she was better off with Harry Crosby after all.

I couldn't forget the look in Rion's eyes. When I'd said goodbye to Harry, I wasn't thinking about him, I was thinking about Rion. I hated hurting anyone's feelings. Except Jas's. And maybe Chad Everett's. Rion had been kind enough to help me, and look how I'd repaid him. I hadn't meant for anything like that to happen.

Life was complicated at times, and when boys were involved, even more so.

I tried to put it out of my mind when I got home. I had a shower and hit the books. I wasn't totally disinterested in getting good marks this year, despite what Kerri thought. I started with chemistry, the bit that Rion had helped me with at lunchtime, and now it all seemed so clear to me I was surprised I hadn't understood it before.

I looked up from my book and out the open door of my room, across the hall to the spare bedroom where Rion had stayed for several months. Without thinking, I got up and went into the room.

It seemed to me that I could almost see him at the desk where he'd spent so much time studying. I sat on the bed and closed my eyes, trying to remember those months. But all I got were images: Rion studying, me sitting here talking to him, sometimes laughing, sometimes arguing, sometimes … I tried, but nothing else came to me. Yet it felt like there should be something more.

Why had he come to stay with us in the first place? I went over what I knew.

I'd met him at the beach last winter when our family had taken a boring holiday. We'd become friends on Facebook. Then he told me that his mum was leaving for Cairns with her boyfriend and he had to stay with his uncle, who lived in our neighbourhood. But when Rion got there, Archimedes had gone on a trip to Brazil.

Mum and Dad said he could stay with us until his uncle returned. Then Archimedes came back and took Rion on his next trip. And now they had both returned for Rion's senior year.

I knew all this, but there was something missing.

I remembered Rion being nerdy, arrogant and unlikeable, but since he'd returned this year, that wasn't the case at all. Yes, he was nerdy, but he also looked pretty hot. (Okay, call me shallow.) Perhaps he could be arrogant, though I hadn't seen any evidence of that yet. And he wasn't unlikeable at all. He had even helped me with my homework.

He seemed nice, so what made me think otherwise?

I hadn't meant to lie when I told him I was busy this afternoon. I just forgot about it when Harry asked me to go for a Coke. I should probably text him. I went back to my room to get my phone.

*Thanks for your help at lunchtime. That chemistry homework makes sense now.*

I waited for a while, but no message came back. Could I blame him? I tried again.

*See you tomorrow.*

I waited again. Looked like Rion wasn't going to answer. Time to put it out of my mind.

I looked at Zoe's texts, debating how to answer. I was glad she'd texted me and I guessed she was trying to say she was sorry. But she probably *had* forgotten that I'd asked her out when she and Harry went to Macca's. And that's what hurt. I'd allowed Archimedes to take away her memories of my alien identity, not just because it would be more convenient all round, but also because I wanted her to be free. I especially wanted her to be free to choose.

And she had. So now I needed to let go.

I put down my phone.

When it buzzed again, I thought it was Zoe, but, to my surprise, it was Jas.

Last year Jas had had a crush on me, but I hadn't given her any encouragement. Even if I hadn't been caught up with Zoe, Jas wasn't the type of person I could ever like. I'd discovered she could be manipulative and unkind at times. But it was the way she treated Zoe that had annoyed me the most. She had used Zoe and then tried to put her down.

When Jas realised I just wasn't interested, she'd turned her attentions back to Chad Everett and had ignored both Zoe and me. So why she did want to get in touch with me now?

*Hey Rion, let's catch up. Coffee, tomorrow after school? Can't wait to hear about Brazil!*

My first instinct was to say no, but then I reconsidered. Jas always had an ulterior motive for doing things. To say I didn't trust her was like saying you didn't trust the hungry tiger in the cage with you. She was plotting something, I felt sure of it. Maybe it would be wise to find out what.

One of my hosts had been a Medici, and that was one of the few times I had learned something from a host. Jas would have fitted in quite well in medieval Italy.

I texted her: *Okay.*

I thought maybe I should sound a little more enthusiastic. I added: *Coffee sounds good.*

As I pressed send, I wondered about Zoe's reaction. I wasn't trying to make her jealous, just because she had hung out with Harry this afternoon. I wouldn't do that. But I had to admit there was a small part of me, perhaps 11.25 percent (maybe even twelve percent), that wouldn't mind if she was a little jealous. However, the main reason was so I could find out what Jas was up to. That was the logical thing to do, wasn't it?

Jas wasn't long in responding to my text. *Cool. Tomorrow then.*

I leaned back in my chair and looked out the window, wondering what chain of events I had just set in motion. Even though I was new at being human, my long existence of alien life had taught me there were consequences to everything, and sometimes they weren't exactly what we expected.

# Chapter Ten

'Hey, Zoe, I really need your advice.'

'Sure, shoot.' I closed my locker and turned to face Lou. She hesitated a moment and I could see she was nervous. 'Come on, Lou, we're friends. Whatever it is, it can't be that bad.'

I was expecting her to ask me about some minor dilemma, such as how she could tell her mum she didn't really want to do tennis or something. Her next sentence surprised me, although it probably shouldn't have.

She let out the breath she'd been holding. 'Okay, here goes,' she said. 'I really like Harry and I just wanted to know how I could get him to notice me more. You're really good at that sort of stuff, you know, with boys and everything.'

Okay, kind of a dilemma here. Harry had asked me out. Just as a friend, but would Lou get that? Should I even tell her? Anyway, Lou was vastly overrating my knowledge about attracting boys. I only had to think about what happened with Chad Everett last year to remind myself of that. Not that I cared any more.

'Sure, Lou, happy to help,' I said, 'not that I know much about it. I'm not Jas, you know.'

'I wouldn't take advice from her even if she offered, which she wouldn't. You're much nicer,' Lou said loyally.

'Lou, I need to tell you something,' I said, feeling uncomfortable.

'What?' Her big blue eyes looked into mine.

I didn't want to kill that look of hope, but I had to be honest. 'Harry and I are going to the movies this weekend.'

'Oh,' she said, and bit her lip.

'But it's not a date or anything. We're just going as friends, that's all,' I said. 'We would have asked you, too, but you said you were going away this weekend.'

'Don't bother to explain. Now that Harry's going out with you he won't give me a second look. I knew he kind of liked you last year, but I didn't think you liked him—not in that way, you know. I also thought that now Rion was here you two would get back together.'

'No, Lou, you've got it all wrong. Harry and I are just friends. He told me that was all he wanted. And as for Rion, we were never together.'

'To be honest, Zoe, that's not what it looked like. And I'm not the only one who thought so. Never mind. I'd better get to class. See ya.'

And after the longest conversation I had ever had with Lou, she turned and quickly headed down the crowded corridor.

Jeez, what was going on? The whole world seemed to think that Rion and I were closer than we were. Obviously, having a boy stay with your family for a few months made everyone jump to conclusions. The wrong ones.

Feeling unsettled, I headed to history class. A lesson on Australia's federation and the relationship between the states and the Commonwealth was just what I needed at the moment to steady my nerves.

It was a long and slightly uncomfortable day. Kerri and I were still not on the best of terms, and Lou was even quieter than usual. Harry was normal, maybe more talkative than usual to me, but that sure didn't help with the impression I wanted to give Lou. I never saw Rion at all. No doubt he was cleaning up the lab, or working in the library or something equally nerdy.

Jas shot me strange looks all day that were a combination of smug and nasty. I ignored them, but I wondered what it was all about. After school, I discovered why.

Heading out the school gates, I saw Rion ahead of me. Maybe he was over what had happened yesterday afternoon. I quickened my pace and had nearly caught up with him when Jas pulled up in her car on the street in front of us. She was older than me and had got her driver's licence during the summer holidays, so naturally her parents had bought her a car. It was a late-model Barina, bright red. An appropriate colour choice, I thought.

Then I saw Rion go up to the curb and hop in the front seat of her car. As they pulled away, I was almost sure I could see Jas's triumphant smile. Why did I care? Why should I care? And yet I discovered to my surprise that I did.

Rion was free to go anywhere with anyone he liked, even if it was Jas. Besides, she had a car. I didn't even have a licence yet. I still needed to get my hours up. And at the rate I was going, I probably never would.

If I had my licence I could go out with my friends in the afternoon, too.

Except that I didn't have a car either, let alone a red one.

And even if I did, I wouldn't be going anywhere with Rion because he'd be with Jas.

And I couldn't go anywhere with Harry because, now that Lou liked him, they'd probably go out together.

*Oh, shut up*, I told myself.

I missed the bus home and had to walk. Some days suck.

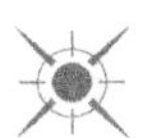

'I know this awesome little coffee place in the Valley. Really good coffee, almost like you'd get in Melbourne. You ever been to Melbourne, Rion?' Jas asked me as we sped away from school. I thought for a moment that I'd seen Zoe behind me when I got into the car. I was already starting to regret going anywhere with Jas.

'Rion?'

'What?' I looked at her, trying to remember what she'd said.

'I said, have you ever been to Melbourne?'

'Um, no.'

'Mum and I go all the time, mainly on shopping trips, especially when Dad's away on business. I've got an aunt there. It's such a cool place. Not at all like Brisbane.'

The light ahead of us had just turned amber. She pushed her foot on the accelerator and we flew through the intersection.

'Is this coffee shop far away?' Hopefully not, I thought.

'Nothing's far away when you can drive. Have you got your licence yet?'

'No,' I said.

'It's so cool … so liberating,' she said, and laughed.

I said nothing, but the closer we got to the city, the heavier the traffic became and the more I noticed that Jas seemed to regard traffic rules as mere guides rather than laws to be followed.

She turned into a parking garage and found a spot on one of the upper levels. She pulled into the parking bay with a screech of tires.

When we got to the coffee shop, she gave me her order and headed for a seat. I ordered for both of us, paid for our drinks and headed to our table with the number thirteen in my hand. Thirteen was supposed to be unlucky; I knew that. But I was a man of science, not superstition.

'So, Rion, here we are together at last, eh?'

'What do you mean?' I was at a complete loss.

'Well, you know we had kind of a thing going last year.'

'Did we?'

She laughed. 'Don't be so shy,' she said, 'I know you liked me. I mean, we even kissed and everything when you were helping me with homework that time. The look on Zoe's face when she came in with those milkshakes was priceless. But she got more than she bargained for, didn't she?' She gave me a wide smile that showed entirely too many teeth. It looked predatory.

The way I remembered it, Jas had kissed me and not the other way around.

'But,' she continued, 'Chad kind of got in the way. He was so into me, you know. I would've had to break his heart when he asked me out if I'd said no. I just couldn't do it. Sorry.' She looked at me with pensive eyes.

'Where is Chad now?' I asked, feeling again like I really shouldn't have said yes to this coffee catch-up.

'Oh, he's away for a few days on a football camp or something like that,' she said, and waved a hand.

Our coffees came. That was good because the sooner we had them, the sooner we could leave.

'Would he mind me having coffee with you?' Maybe I could remind her that she did, after all, have a boyfriend.

'Would he?' she looked at me, raising an eyebrow. 'That's an interesting question, isn't it? Should he mind, Rion? You tell me.' She leaned towards me and I was engulfed in a waft of perfume.

I sat back, trying to put as much distance as I could between us. 'No, not at all, not one little bit.'

She gave me a look that could only be described as calculating. 'I think that kind of depends.'

'On what?' I knew I shouldn't have asked that question.

'On what's happening between you and Zoe. You're not staying with her family anymore, so you're not under any obligation to her or anything.'

'Nothing's happening between Zoe and me,' were the unwise words I said. They were out before I knew it and it was too late to take them back.

'Well, that's good to know,' she said. 'Because, Rion, I've always liked you. And you think I'm pretty, don't you?' Jas put her hands under her chin and looked at me with her clear blue eyes.

Making a strictly objective observation, I had to say she was what most people would call good-looking. She had long blonde hair, perfectly symmetrical features, and a wide smile that revealed straight white teeth. But her looks did nothing for me. Perhaps that's because I was an alien. But that didn't explain why I much preferred Zoe's round face, large brown eyes and dark brown curly hair. To me, Zoe was beautiful.

Her eyes held mine. I tried to be honest. 'Yes, of course, everyone knows you're attractive.' I meant it entirely in the objective sense, but it came out all wrong.

Another smile. 'How sweet of you to say that. So, Rion, the question is, where do we go from here?'

*Nowhere*, my mind shouted, *nowhere at all*. But I found myself saying, 'What do you mean?'

'Oh, Rion, you're too cute at times. You know exactly what I mean. You can have it all if you want. Good grades, popularity *and* me. We're suited, you know. We'd make such an awesome couple. It's fate. We were meant to be together. We're both alphas.'

I was about to protest when she said, 'Hush. Don't say a word or you'll ruin it. You know, of course, that I'm just talking hypothetically. But it's something for you to consider. When you're alone in bed at night, think about this.'

She leaned forward and pressed her lips against mine. Jas had kissed me once before, but this time it was different. She moved her lips against mine slowly, rhythmically, with a pressure that was not unpleasant. I didn't mean to, I didn't want to, but somehow I think I responded, a little.

Then she moved away and gave a little laugh. 'Wow, you'll do. And now I think we'd better go, before we lead each other astray. Besides, I've got a zumba class tonight.'

*No one's leading anyone astray* was what I wanted to say to her, but the words never got out. We got up and left our barely touched coffees behind.

The drive back was probably just as crazy as the drive there, but I didn't notice it as much. When Jas pulled up in front of my house with a screech of tires, I felt dizzy. Whether it was from the kiss or the drive, I wasn't quite sure.

'I'll see you tomorrow, Rion. And you know what? If you play your cards right, I might just let you take me out sometime.'

I got out of the car, feeling overwhelmed. As she took off in a cloud of exhaust, I wondered what had just happened to me. And then I realised something. Not once had she asked me about my trip to Brazil.

'So, Mum and Dad, which of you guys is going to take me on a driving lesson? I've had my learner's permit since before Christmas and we've hardly gone out at all.' I looked at them both over my spaghetti bolognaise. The spaghetti was mushy and overcooked. Mum's brief success in cooking had been just that—brief. It was almost comforting to know she hadn't really changed.

'We've been busy over the summer holidays, and you were in Sydney for a month. There hasn't been a lot of time,' Mum said, as she passed the salad to Dad.

'According to my logbook, I've done ten hours. Only another ninety to go. You know I was hoping to get my licence before I got my old-age pension.'

'Ha-ha, very funny,' Dad said. 'I'm sure Mum will take you one afternoon this week, when she isn't busy.'

Mum speared him with a look. 'And how many hours have you taken Zoe out?'

He looked uncomfortable. 'I'm not sure, but I do get home late.'

'Zero hours, that's how many,' Mum said. 'And you could take her at night. She does need to get some night driving in.'

'Yeah,' I said, 'we could go tonight, Dad.'

'Don't you have studying or something to do?'

'Did it this afternoon after school,' I said, shooting him a smug smile. I was prepared and determined. I was really over the fact that everyone else seemed to have their licence and I didn't. Well, Jas anyway.

'Tonight sounds like a great idea. I'll clear up,' Mum said, 'so you can go as soon as we finish dinner.'

Dad was cornered and he knew it. 'Okay. But we're only going locally, not into the city. After all, it is night time and you haven't had a lot of experience driving in the dark.'

Whatever, I thought. I just wanted to get my hours up and I didn't much care where we went.

Once we were in the car, Dad started to give me about a million instructions.

'Slow down, Dad, I can only do one thing at a time. And besides, I do know how to drive. I just need the experience.'

'Experience is everything. Put your indicator on and don't go too fast,' Dad said as I started the engine. 'And check your mirrors!'

I slid into the dark, quiet street where traffic, this time of night, was practically non-existent.

I was actually not a bad driver. Gran had been showing me how to drive since I was fifteen, before I had my learner's permit. When I visited her in Sydney we would sometimes go on drives to the country, and last year she decided she'd show me how to drive. We just didn't mention it to Mum and Dad, who would have freaked if they'd known. Gran was cool like that. She said she'd learned to drive on the farm when she was twelve, and the earlier you learned the better as far as she was concerned.

Dad, unlike Gran, was anything but cool. 'Careful, you're too close to the white line.'

'I'm going to turn here at the next left,' I said.

'Put your indicator on. Slow down, slow down, SLOW DOWN!' His eyes were riveted on the street we were turning into. Not a car was in sight.

'Chill, I know how to turn a corner.' I expertly changed gears and swung into the street. I noticed he was pressing an imaginary brake with his left foot.

'You're overconfident, Zoe, and that causes accidents. Okay, at the end of this street turn left, and this time try not to jerk me out of my seat as we turn.' Dad was not a patient person at the best of times, but usually he was pretty easy to get on with. I say usually, because as a driving instructor he was like a weightlifter on steroids.

'Zoe, did you see that red light? Seriously, did you see it? Because you could've fooled me.' He turned to face me, his forehead all wrinkled with worry and his brown eyes piercing mine.

'I stopped in time. I didn't go through it or anything.'

'No, you stopped at the last moment and we just about flew through the windscreen. Pull over, pull over, pull over.'

I put on the indicator, moved smoothly to the curb and put the car in park. Turning to face Dad, I said, trying to be calm, 'Now what?'

'Maybe I should drive home,' he said, unclenching his hand from the grip he'd had on the armrest.

'We've hardly been out half an hour. That's not much help.'

'We can say it was an hour.'

'That would be lying, and as you know, totally wrong.' It was so good when you could use your parents' arguments against them.

He gave a heavy sigh and lifted a hand to his head, brushing back his short brown hair. I wondered if it would have a few more greys after tonight. 'All right, just give me a moment to calm my nerves.'

I looked at the street sign, lit up by the streetlight next to it. 'Hey, this is where Rion and his uncle live,' I said. Actually, I knew that. I had, sort of, headed in this direction deliberately. I was just curious, that was all. And part of me wondered if I would see a red Barina outside his place. Not that I cared or anything.

'Oh yes, well, we wouldn't want to drop in on them unannounced or anything,' Dad said.

As I looked over at the row of townhouses, I remembered the run I'd taken here, just before Rion came back to school. And then it hit me. That figure I'd seen in the window, it must have been him. I remembered feeling … something. Bizarre. I wished I could figure it out.

'Dad,' I said, 'what do you think of Rion?'

He looked at me in surprise. 'You know Mum and I both like him. I have to admit I had my reservations when he first came to stay. But he proved me wrong. He was polite, helpful and very thoughtful at times. It would be hard not to like him. He was really good for you, too.'

'What do you mean?'

'He encouraged you to study more, got you away from some of those unsuitable friends you had last year … Why are you asking me this? You know what he's like. You spent enough time together.'

'Did we?'

'What's wrong with you, Zoe? Of course you did. And he even planned that birthday surprise for you in the hot-air balloon.'

'So that was his idea?'

'Yes, and that was the last day he was with us, remember? His uncle came for him that evening and whisked him away.

But the less I say about that Archimedes fellow the better. Honestly, this driving lesson must have rattled your brains or something. I know it has mine.'

He looked at his watch. 'Come on, let's get going again. And for goodness' sake, Zoe, look where you're going and obey the road signs, especially the speed limit.'

After another agonising half hour, we went home. When I pulled into the driveway I think we were both relieved.

'Dad, I think you're probably too tired to take me on driving lessons at night.' I was trying to be diplomatic.

'Yes, dear,' he said, quick to agree with me. 'And let's be honest, your mum is more patient than me.'

'Just a little.' I smiled. 'But you know Mum's busy, too, and I'd really like to get my driver's licence this year. Maybe I could take lessons from a driving school.'

'They're pretty expensive.' As an accountant, Dad was always careful with money, not that he was tight or anything.

'Well, if I had a job I could pay for them myself.'

'You know how we feel about that. It's really important that you concentrate on your studies. Especially this year. '

'But I haven't had any babysitting jobs for ages.'

Dad thought for a moment. 'Well, I'll ask around at work and see if anyone needs a good babysitter. And maybe I could pay for half of your lessons and you could pay for the other half, or something like that.'

I sighed. It was better than nothing. 'Okay. I just hope you have a lot of friends with babies.'

When we went inside, Mum looked up from the papers she was correcting. 'Well, how did it go?'

I could finally say what I'd been holding in the last hour. 'Dad is a terrible driving instructor. I'm only going out with you in the future, Mum, or someone who's qualified.'

Dad only said, 'I think I need a drink.'

# Chapter Eleven

Harry Crosby had always been in my life, and most of the time I'd taken him for granted. When we were little we'd played in backyard wading pools and the sandpit at kindy. We'd gone to each other's birthday parties over the years. Sometimes, because our mums were friends, our families went camping together.

Harry was a pal. He'd always been there for me and I'd tried to be there for him—most of the time. Neither of us had been what you'd call cool. I'd been skinny and a bit of a tomboy. Harry had been about half a centimetre shorter than me, and while not exactly fat, he could've been called comfortably plump. We joked around, hung out sometimes and were totally comfortable around each other.

Until last year.

Last year I'd become a 'cool' kid, and hung out with Jas and her group. I went to parties (even some that Mum and Dad didn't know about), wore heavy makeup, pretended to drink a lot (which I hardly ever did), and started to take boys seriously (my experiences in that area were highly exaggerated).

My social life went up, but my marks went down. I wasn't always the nicest or easiest person to get along with. But Harry had stuck by me through all of that and I wouldn't let anyone put him down, not even the kids in Jas's group. I even got him invited to a party or two. But then Harry had got serious and I didn't. We'd been awkward with each other ever since he'd tried to kiss me at the family barbecue last year.

Now, with Harry's transformation, things between us had changed again. It wasn't just that Harry looked good; he'd changed inside, too. He was more confident and more assertive, and I didn't think of him as just someone I'd played with in the sandpit anymore.

Sometimes when he looked at me, I wondered what I'd do if he tried to kiss me again. Would I turn my head away this time? But we were just friends. That's what he wanted. That's what I wanted.

Wasn't it?

When our doorbell rang, I tried to ignore the nervous feeling inside me. Get over it, I told myself. It's only Harry.

I heard Mum's voice downstairs. 'Hi, Harry, come on in. My goodness, haven't you grown over the summer.'

I headed downstairs before Mum could give him the third degree or say something really embarrassing, as only she could do.

Harry's eyes caught mine. There was a look in them I hadn't seen before. In that moment I knew for certain that the Harry I used to know had grown up. The awkward, shy boy I once knew had disappeared for good. And it wasn't just the tight jeans he wore instead of cargo pants, or the cool green shirt that matched his hazel eyes, or the slightly longer haircut that was no longer his usual straight back and sides.

It was something else. Or maybe it wasn't just Harry. Maybe it was me, too. Maybe we had both grown up.

'Hey,' I said, as I went down to meet him.

'You look amazing,' he said.

'Thanks. You look pretty cool, too.'

Mum beamed at us. 'Well, have fun, you two. I know I don't have to remind you, Harry, that Zoe should be home by midnight.'

I rolled my eyes. Talk about overprotective. It was *Harry*, for God's sake.

'No worries, Mrs Brennan, I'll have her home on time.' He turned to me. 'Mum lent me the car tonight.'

'You have your licence now?' Did everyone in senior year have a licence except me?

'Yeah, remember I turned seventeen during the school holidays. Uncle Adrian helped me get my hours up.'

I looked pointedly at Mum. 'Do you realise how many hours of practice we have to do before my birthday, Mum? And don't go palming me off on Dad. I don't want to go with him anymore, remember? Did he tell you about our plan for proper driving lessons?'

She laughed over her shoulder as she headed back to the lounge room. 'Yes, he did. But you never know, he might improve with practice.'

'I don't want to test that theory,' I said.

Harry and I walked to his mum's late-model Camry, and he even opened the door for me. Very smooth, but it was starting to feel a little date-like, which it absolutely wasn't.

Trying to keep it light, I said, 'I can drive pretty well, you know. Gran taught me last year when I went to Sydney. And if you can drive in Sydney, you can drive anywhere, trust me.'

He grinned. 'Yeah, maybe,' he said, and started the car, 'but I seem to remember you tried to drive your dad's SUV on one of our family camping trips and we nearly ended up in Somerset Dam. Thank God the brakes worked and your parents never found out.'

'Hey, I was only thirteen. I've improved a lot since then,' I protested, but I had to laugh, too. In those days I was in the habit of doing things that shocked Harry. I wondered if he was still as shockable.

'Yeah? I wondered if that was why your dad doesn't want to take you out.'

I gave him a light punch on the arm. 'Hey, whose side are you on?'

'Yours, always.' He gave me a glance that melted me inside.

'Well, that's good to know,' I mumbled, and looked out the window.

When we arrived at the movies, I found that Harry had prepaid tickets. 'No way, Harry,' I protested, 'we're here as friends. I'll pay you for my ticket.'

He shrugged. 'Don't worry about it,' he said. 'You can get them next time.'

'Then I'll get the popcorn.' I was determined to pay for something.

'Well, make sure you get two so you don't eat all of mine like you usually do.'

'I do not. Only once, years ago—jeez, memory like an elephant.'

The movie was great. Harry and I had watched the original Star Wars movies on DVD over the years and we were both confirmed fans. As we sat there making the occasional comment to each other it was just like old times.

When we walked out afterwards, he said, 'Do you want to go for a cold drink or something? We've got time. It's only ten o'clock.'

'Honestly, Mum and her curfews.'

'It's good that she cares, right? And we've still got a couple of hours.'

Outside the cineplex, the bistros and cafes were humming with the usual Friday-night buzz of people and chatter. We went to one of the cafes and sat at a table outside. I looked at the menu.

Harry looked at me and smiled. 'Go on, I know you want the ice chocolate with sprinkles.'

I lifted my chin and said, 'I was actually considering either a long black or a skinny latte.'

This time he snorted. 'You were not,' he said. 'You always used to order an ice chocolate when we came to the mall after school.'

'I believe I was in middle school then. My tastes have matured, you know.'

He shook his head. 'Some things never change. Just have what you want, Zoe.'

I sighed. 'Oh, all right, and I may as well have an extra scoop of ice cream. But I'll totally blame you if I get fat.'

'That's something you'll never have to worry about. Not like me,' he said with a rueful look.

I felt a rush of sympathy for him. 'Hey, you look great,' I said, covering my hand with his. 'Don't put yourself down.'

'But I had to work at it,' he said, 'and I still do. I go to the gym nearly every day and can never eat the way I used to again. Not that I want to or anything. And I'm not looking for pity so stop looking at me like that. It was all worth it. Especially now.' He turned my hand over in his, giving it a squeeze.

'Well, you were always nice on the inside, Harry.'

As we looked at each other, I realised that something in both of us had changed. We were still Harry and Zoe, pals, but it seemed like we'd taken a step towards something else. It kind of scared me, because I didn't know if I wanted to go in that direction or not.

The ice chocolate was almost as good as I remembered, but somehow my stomach just wasn't in the mood for it. Harry must have sensed my nervousness, because he started to talk, bringing up old memories of when we were kids and the crazy things we used to do. Well, mainly me. He got me laughing and I forgot all the other stuff that was swirling around in my brain.

But on the way home, in the silence of the car, it came back to me. And when he parked the car in front of my house, it was there hanging in the air between us. We weren't kids anymore and I wasn't just going to punch him lightly on the arm and say, 'See ya tomorrow, Harry.' It wasn't going to be that simple.

When we walked to the door, Harry said, 'Hey, thanks for coming out with me tonight, Zoe. I had a great time with you.'

'Yeah, it was fun.' I forced myself to look at him.

He reached out a hand and stroked my cheek. He was going to kiss me, I knew it. And this time I knew I wouldn't turn my head. I closed my eyes and waited. And waited.

And then his hand dropped. 'You'd better go in,' he said. 'You don't want to be late. After all, it's nearly midnight and I wouldn't want you to be a minute late or anything.' He gave a small laugh.

I opened my eyes and took a step back. My face was hot, and I was sure it must be red.

'Call you tomorrow?' he said, as if he hadn't noticed I'd made a complete fool of myself.

I nodded, not trusting myself to speak.

'Maybe we can do something,' he said.

'Maybe.' I wasn't going to act all enthusiastic or anything, not now.

'Great,' he said and gave me a smile. Then he turned and headed down the path to his car.

I slipped inside. Mum and Dad had gone to bed, but they'd left the downstairs light on for me. If it had been any other boy, I'm sure Mum would have stayed up, just in case. But I knew she wasn't worried about Harry. She trusted him.

I reached my bedroom and flopped down on my bed. Why oh why had I thought Harry was going to kiss me? It was super-embarrassing. Here I was thinking something was happening between us when it absolutely wasn't. Harry had meant what he said. He just wanted to be friends. How could I have read it so wrong?

And then a vision flashed into my mind. It was a kiss that had actually happened. I remembered the feeling so strongly, and I also remembered that it nearly broke my heart. But I couldn't remember when or even who it had been. It hadn't been Harry, and it couldn't have been Rion. But if not either of them, who? Nothing made sense to me.

I decided I must have been imagining things. Either that, or I was going crazy. Distinct possibility.

As I lay in the dark, trying to figure things out, I heard the ping of my phone with a text. I knew it was Harry, but I couldn't bring myself to look at it yet. I wasn't ready. I needed to figure things out, but what those things were … I wished I knew.

# Chapter Twelve

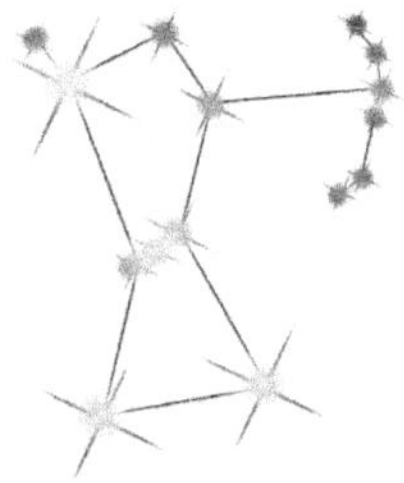

I looked in the mirror in disbelief and horror. There was an ugly red blemish on my chin. What was happening to me? It was obviously something serious. I thought carefully about the last few days. I hadn't done anything to cause this.

I knew, when I decided to remain human, that my body would be subject to all the conditions and drawbacks of a physical body. But after Archimedes had pointed out my slight weight gain and muscle loss, I had improved my diet and exercise program.

Leaning closer to the mirror, I looked at this imperfection on my skin more carefully. Touching it gently, I winced at the unexpected pain. A feeling of panic set in. Maybe this was just the beginning. I might start to develop other malfunctions in this physical body of mine. Soon I might get other spots, develop a fever, a contagious disease. Or worse, suffer heart or kidney failure.

This could be the start of a total physical breakdown. Perhaps my people had got it all wrong. Maybe I couldn't stay human after all and I'd have to return to my former state before things got worse.

My mind raced in twenty different directions. No doubt about it, this was an emergency, code red. I needed to contact Archimedes urgently before something more drastic happened.

I closed my eyes and initiated the telepathic connection, making sure I entered the correct digital sequence that would indicate a dire emergency. Then I went downstairs, sat on the couch and waited.

And waited.

Did Archimedes not realise the seriousness of the situation? Couldn't they have given me a more reliable guardian? I could have died while I waited. It was three minutes and thirty-five seconds before he materialised before me.

'What's wrong?' he said. 'Has World War III been declared? Is an environmental disaster of epic proportions about to erupt?' He looked more annoyed than concerned. Archimedes was not an empathetic being.

'No, something more important, I think I'm dying. And you took long enough to get here.'

He looked closely at me, using the power of his enhanced eyesight to assess my physical condition. 'You look fine. I can't detect any malfunctions in your body. Oh, you have a pimple on your chin. I did warn you about your diet.'

'Exactly. I have a blemish. I had a perfect body, which has now begun to break down. This is only the beginning. My body is beginning to deteriorate. No doubt I'll develop other symptoms very soon. You need to do something, Archimedes. You need to help me.'

Archimedes collapsed on the sofa beside me. 'I really don't know why I volunteered for this job. I was led to believe it would be much easier. Just enrol you in school, pop in now and again to check on you and that would be it. I never realised you would be so needy.' He closed his eyes.

'Needy?' I looked at him in disbelief. 'I'm *dying*.'

'Well, of course you are,' he said, opening his eyes. 'But don't blame me, you're the one who chose to be human. It stands to reason that an organic body will start to deteriorate almost from the moment it enters the world. Especially in this world, where there's so much pollution and people on bad diets with unhealthy lifestyles. I shouldn't be at all surprised if you expired before you were forty.'

He shrugged. 'But you can't say you weren't warned. You could have chosen to return to the perfection of your former bodiless, intelligent existence, where you would have thrived for the next few thousand years. I've never understood why you made such an obviously poor choice to remain human. But there it is. Now, if that's all I'll be off.' He rose from the sofa.

I pulled on his arm and he sank onto the sofa again.

'Really, Orion, there's no need for such physical manhandling.'

'Didn't you hear what I said, you pompous windbag?'

If those eyes could have tasered me, they would have. But at least I'd got his attention. 'I don't mean I might die in the next twenty or thirty years, I meant it's happening *now*. You do realise that in human terms I have a seventeen-year-old body. That's much too young to die.'

'You're not dying at the moment, though right at this moment I'm inclined to hasten the process.'

He looked down at my hand still on his arm. I dropped it. No point in antagonising him too much, especially since I needed his help.

'You're merely experiencing the effects of adolescence due to your hormones,' he continued. 'Sometimes it comes a little earlier, but it's not unusual for a teenager to get the odd pimple or two. It will clear up in time.'

'You mean this is normal?'

He nodded. 'More or less. It differs from one individual to another, but it's relatively common and not life threatening in the least. Surely you knew this.'

'Yes, but I never really thought such a condition would affect me.' I sat back against the couch, not sure if I felt relieved or simply confused.

'Why not? You're human now. You will age, you will be subject to colds, influenza and in time wrinkles and possibly arthritis. You might even become bald. Oh, the delights that await you.'

He laughed and stood up again. 'And now I really must go. You've wasted enough of my time. Next time you signal an emergency, make sure it's worthwhile, like nuclear disaster or something. Well, adieu,' he said. And within less time than it took me to blink, he'd disappeared.

I wasn't dying. That was a relief. But now another problem confronted me. How was I going to face the world with this ugly red spot on my chin? I thought of Zoe. She didn't have the highest opinion of me as it was and now it would only get worse.

I headed for the bathroom again, where there was a first-aid kit, one of the few things Archimedes had stocked the house with. He'd obviously had more foresight than me because it had never occurred to me I would need such a thing.

Opening the metal container, I took out bandages, antiseptic cream, tape, Mercurochrome and a small package of Band-Aids. The bandages were too large, the cream did nothing to hide the blemish, and the Mercurochrome left a rusty stain on my hand when I tested it. At least I hadn't put it on my chin first. That only left the packet of Band-Aids. Opening it up, I saw they were far too large to be of help on a spot that could be measured in millimetres rather than centimetres.

I put everything back in the box, went into my bedroom and sat on the edge of my bed, trying to think.

Surely someone who had lived as long as I had, and who had accumulated such a vast amount of knowledge over the millennia, would know what to do about a pimple. I considered a doctor, but according to Archimedes' it was a minor condition only. Perhaps I had overreacted—a little. Then I thought of a pharmacy. Maybe I'd find something there.

I took the bus to the local shopping centre, pleased to be doing something constructive. I was conscious of my pimple all the way there and was sure everyone I passed noticed it. How could they miss it?

When I got to the pharmacy, I headed straight to the counter. A woman in a cherry-red top with the words *Chem Mart* on the pocket came up to me. 'May I help you?'

'Um, I have a problem.'

'What is it?'

I wondered if she was visually impaired. I pointed to my chin. 'I need something for this.'

'Oh, you want an acne cream. We have several here. I'll just go get them.' She turned and went away to the shelves.

'Hi, Rion.'

Usually I'd be happy to hear that voice, but not today. And definitely not here. Cupping my hand over my chin and folding my arms in what I hoped was a casual pose, I turned around. 'Hi, Zoe.'

Her expression was cool. What had I done? And then I remembered that the last time I saw her I was getting into Jas's car. Maybe that was it. For the eighty-seventh time, I wished I hadn't gone anywhere with Jas. Big mistake.

'How are you?' I asked politely, still keeping the hand on my chin.

'Fine,' she said.

Not a promising start. 'That's good. I'm fine too.' I said, which wasn't exactly true. 'What are you doing here?' As soon as I said it I realised it was a stupid question because now she would ask me what I was doing here and I would have to tell her.

'Just picking up something for Mum.' She turned away to ask a shop assistant for some headache tablets. I got the feeling she didn't want to talk to me.

Then the woman who was serving me came back with several boxes in her hand. 'Here are several of our most popular brands of acne treatments,' she said in a booming voice. 'Would you be looking for a treatment only, a treatment and concealment, or maybe just something to cover it over? I recommend the second one. Most people your age find it very effective.'

'That one will be fine,' I said, not wanting to prolong this any further. I could easily have dematerialised into a bodiless, alien entity right in that moment if the choice were given to me.

'That'll be fourteen ninety-five,' she said.

I passed her a twenty and she went to get my change. Then I stole a look at Zoe, forgetting to put my hand on my chin.

'Good choice,' she said, looking straight at my chin. 'Better to act sooner rather than later.'

I was surprised that she hadn't recoiled in horror. At least she'd talked to me. But she was turning to leave. I had to do something, say something.

'Zoe, about that coffee with Jas, I didn't really want to go,' I blurted out.

She faced me again, and I noticed her cheeks were red. 'Oh, you had coffee with Jas? It doesn't concern me, Rion. Why should it?' She shrugged. 'Oh, by the way, you might want to take your change.'

I turned to where the shop assistant was holding out my packet and change. 'Thanks,' I said, taking it.

When I turned back, Zoe was heading out the door. I rushed after her. 'I'm glad you don't mind because it meant nothing,' I said. 'I thought she might be up to something, and if she was, I wanted to find out. I know she's hurt you in the past and I didn't want it happening again.' I was suddenly aware of how crazy I sounded.

She stopped. 'Really?' She looked at me. 'That sounds a bit … extreme. Besides, you don't have to worry about me. I'm capable of looking after myself.'

'I know. I can be like that at times. You know, not normal. But I guess I can't help myself looking out for you. It's a habit.' I smiled at her and for the first time that afternoon, I saw the beginnings of a smile from her.

'A habit? Since when?'

'Since I stayed with you and your family. We were good friends then, Zoe.'

'Were we?'

I wanted to say more, but even if I did, I knew she wouldn't believe me. So all I said was, 'Yes. We spent a lot of time together.'

'Oh.' She was silent for a moment and then she said, 'I guess I owe you an explanation, too. That day I was with Harry at Macca's … I'm sorry, but I completely forgot you asked me to go to the mall with you. And the Harry thing, it was just a spur-of-the-moment idea. We didn't stay long. I'm sorry if I hurt you.'

'It's okay,' I said, and now it was.

We stared at each other, smiling, for 3.25 seconds, which is actually a long time.

'Well, did she?' Zoe asked.

'Pardon?' This time I was the one who was confused.

'Did Jas have any devious plans for me?'

'Oh, no.' I wasn't going to tell her that Jas's plans had more to do with me. It didn't matter because they weren't going to happen. 'And I'd much rather have coffee with you. That would be far colder—I mean cooler.' My tongue was tripping up on me.

This time Zoe's face did break into a smile. 'You haven't made that mistake in a while. Not since last year.'

I gave a nervous laugh. 'That's true. And at least I don't wear pink socks any more.'

'Oh yeah, I forgot about that. Your fashion sense has definitely improved.'

'Thanks to you. I seem to remember you tried to stop me buying a large Hawaiian shirt.' It had been my first shopping excursion ever, and Zoe had actually lent me money to buy some clothes for my new human life.

'You had terrible taste back then,' she said, and laughed.

I laughed with her and started to feel more relaxed. Perhaps having a pimple wasn't the disaster it had seemed. 'So, are you free now? We could hang out, do something.'

She shook her head. 'Sorry, I'm just about to meet someone. Some other time, hey? See you at school on Monday then.' She gave me another smile and walked away.

*Someone*. That one word sent me from happy to depressed. I had a feeling I knew who that someone was. But just because she was meeting him again didn't necessarily mean anything, I told myself. Zoe and Harry had been friends for years.

Who was I kidding? Harry was actually a nice guy. And now that he'd improved himself, he looked like the kind of boy Zoe should be with. She liked him. And at the moment he looked an awful lot better than me. Why would she give me even a second glance?

I had lived for over four thousand years and had been, via my hosts, through many experiences. But not once, in all that time, had I ever thought that being a human teenager would be so hard.

# Chapter Thirteen

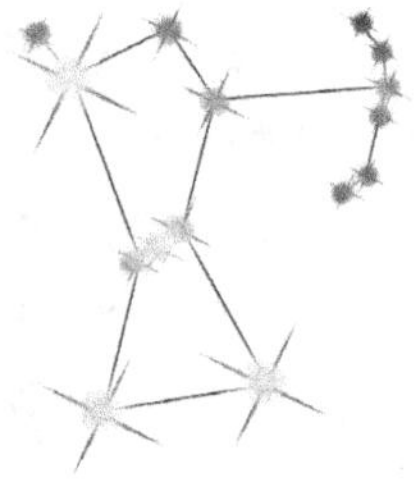

What was wrong with me? Why were all my memories about Rion so confused?

Up till now, I'd forgotten that I'd gone shopping with him last year. Now I was getting flashbacks, like bits of a movie that didn't make sense. Rion had been totally hopeless about even the most basic items of clothing. I'd even had to remind him to buy socks and underwear—and then he went and bought the pink socks. Why had he been so strange back then? He seemed pretty normal to me now.

There were so many gaps in my memory about what had happened last year that it was starting to worry me. What was happening to me? And, more importantly, what happened to me last year that I couldn't remember?

And my confusion was making me all mixed up about my feelings for Harry. I liked the new Harry. But what if I'd also liked Rion at one point? But even if I had, I told myself firmly, that was in the past. This was now.

So, my brain spinning with these thoughts, I walked into the cafe and over to where Harry was sitting. 'Hey,' I said, as I slid into the seat opposite him.

Harry looked great. His T-shirt stretched across his now broad chest and his hair was just that bit longer than last year. I felt, well, just a little bit fluttery and even more confused.

'Hi,' Harry said, 'glad you could make it.'

'Yeah, well, it was either this or studying, so no contest.' I gave an awkward laugh.

'Gee, thanks, good to know I rank above maths and history.' He smiled. 'I had fun last night.'

'Me, too.' *Except when I acted like a fool and thought you were going to kiss me.* Didn't share that out loud.

'We should do it again sometime.'

I played with the fringe on my bag. 'Yeah, we should. Maybe Kerri and Lou can make it next time.' I still felt guilty about Lou, knowing how she felt about Harry.

'Maybe,' he said. 'Or we could just go out together.' He quirked an eyebrow.

'You mean as friends?' I wanted things to be perfectly clear between us.

'Yeah, we could go out as friends. Or even … on a date.' He hesitated for a moment and then added, 'a real one.' He shrugged, as if it made no difference to him.

I wasn't sure what to say. After last night I didn't want to appear too eager. He certainly didn't seem to be.

'No rush,' Harry said, 'just think about it. Anyway, we should order.'

I picked up the menu. 'And I'm not having an ice chocolate today,' I said, happy to change the subject. 'That was just a one-off, for old times' sake. Today, I'm a totally mature senior who's going to have a long black.'

'Seriously? Not even a cappuccino? With chocolate powder sprinkled on top?'

I closed the menu with a snap. 'Seriously,' I said, and grinned.

'In that case, I'll have the same. I'll order,' he said, starting to get up.

'Hang on. Sit down. I'm getting this one. You got the movie tickets last night.'

'You got the pop—'

I cut him off before he could say anymore. 'And now I'm getting the coffee. No arguments. Besides, I've got a babysitting job this week, I'll be in the money.'

He gave me a half smile. 'Do I have a choice?'

'Not this time, maybe next time.'

We managed to keep everything light, and were soon back to being comfortable with each other—nearly. There was still an awkward vibe between us, almost as if we didn't quite know where we fit with each other anymore.

We left the cafe and Harry walked me home.

'So, Monday at school, hey,' he said. 'Maybe we could catch a cola after school one day this week.'

'Yeah, maybe, see ya,' I said, and slipped inside the door. No way was I going to let him think I was waiting for a kiss *this* time.

'Zoe, is that you?' Mum called from the lounge room.

'No, it's your passionate admirer, Archimedes, who thinks you outshine them all,' I said, as I dumped my bag on the side table near the door.

Mum came out and gave me a look. 'Very funny.'

'I thought so.'

'Well, have you and your sense of humour remembered it's your turn to cook tonight? You did volunteer.'

'Me and my big mouth. Okay, frozen pizza coming up.'

'I think there were promises made of something a little more exciting, such as chicken parmigiana or veal with mushroom cream sauce.'

'Seriously? This from a lady who thinks that spaghetti Bolognaise is gourmet dining,' I said, heading towards the kitchen.

Mum followed me. 'I hope you haven't forgotten my beef Wellington already.'

I stopped and turned around. 'That was amazing, Mum, I still don't know how you did it.'

'I was inspired. And now I can rest on my reputation for the next five years at least.'

'And you know for sure that Rion's uncle liked it,' I said, moving to the fridge and peeking inside to see what was there.

Mum sighed. 'He certainly did. Poor Rion, I do feel for him, having such an odd guardian.'

'He's weird, all right.' I wrinkled my nose at the thought of cooking anything from scratch. 'Mum, do you think we could have tacos tonight?'

'Sounds perfect, and why don't we make them together? It'll be more fun that way. You do the chicken and I'll cut up the salad things.'

'You sure? I thought you had marking or something to do.'

Mum reached down to the crisper to get out the lettuce and tomatoes. 'Darling, I've always got marking to do. If I let that get in the way, I'd never do anything.' She went over to the bench top and got out the knife and cutting board. 'You know, I think we should invite Rion over again, maybe after school or something. That way we wouldn't have to inconvenience his uncle or anything.'

'You mean we wouldn't have to invite him,' I said, getting out the chicken and the frying pan.

'Something like that,' Mum said, smiling. 'Also, we never really got much of a chance to talk to Rion. Your dad and I miss him, you know. He was like family when he stayed with us. I just want to make sure he's okay and that things are going well for him.'

'Like family? Mum, he just stayed with us for a short time.' I turned to look at her. Yet another example of how everyone remembered things differently than I did.

Mum gave me a look of surprise. 'How can you say that, Zoe? You and Rion were such good friends. He helped you so much with your studies, and he shared the chores around the house. He even planned your birthday.'

'Oh, I guess I just forgot.' Trying not to show how upset I was, I turned back to the stove and started to fry the chicken tenderloins.

Mum began to cut up the tomatoes. 'How about Wednesday? He could come home with you after school and stay for dinner. That would be nice, wouldn't it? Just like old times.'

*No.*

I wasn't sure if I was ready for that, and I wasn't even sure if Rion was, either. How could it be like old times if I didn't know what old times were?

I made a noncommittal grunt and continued with the chicken.

But Mum wouldn't let it go. 'Great. I'll just mention it to Dad, but I'm sure he'd be delighted to see Rion. You can ask him when you see him at school on Monday. I'm so glad we decided on this.'

We hadn't decided on anything, but I let that go. When my mum set her mind on something, it was hard to change it.

The next day I waited until I could catch Rion alone after class. I hadn't wanted to ask him when we were having lunch together in case everyone got the wrong impression. After all, this was more my mum's invitation than mine.

'Hey, Rion, wait up,' I said, walking to the door after him.

He turned and waited, holding the door open for me. 'Hi, Zoe, you want to speak to me?'

'I was wondering if you were free on Wednesday afternoon.'

He looked surprised. 'I guess so. Why?'

He stopped under the shade of a tree and everyone streamed past us to buses and waiting cars. He was looking at me with a peculiar expression on his face. Oh God, it was like I could read his mind.

'I'm not asking you out or anything,' I blurted out without thinking. And then I stopped. I'd only made matters worse. I felt my cheeks burning and I could see the colour rising in his face, too.

'I mean, what I should've said is that my mum wanted to know if you'd like to have dinner with us. You could come home with me after school, if you wanted to.' Could I have been any more clumsy? Jeez.

He was quiet for a moment, and then he said, 'That's nice of her, but I'm not sure if my uncle can make it that night.'

'Oh, he's not invited.' I'd done it again. I seemed to have a bad case of foot-in-mouth disease. I bit my lip and tried once more.

'Not that he wouldn't be welcome or anything, but Mum thought maybe you'd like to come by yourself so we could catch up. They didn't really get a chance to talk to you much when you came with Archimedes. And we wouldn't want to inconvenience him. His time must be valuable, being a photojournalist and all.'

Rion's mouth quirked up in a crooked grin. All of a sudden my stomach gave a flip. How could I have forgotten what a great smile he had?

'It's sometimes hard for other people to talk when Archimedes is around. He does tend to demand attention.'

I had to smile back. 'He sure is an interesting person.'

'That's a very diplomatic way of putting it. But to answer your question, yes, I'd love to come to dinner. Will Harry be there, too?'

I looked at him in puzzlement. 'Harry? Why would he be there?'

He hesitated before saying, 'I had the impression you two were … together.'

'Um, we hang out sometimes, sure. We're just friends.' To tell the truth, I wasn't sure *what* Harry and I were anymore. Not that I was going to say that to Rion.

'Oh, I see.' His tone was neutral, but did I detect relief in his expression?

'Anyway, I'll let Mum know.' I shifted my bag to my other arm. 'I better let you go before you miss your bus.'

'Okay, well, tell your parents I'm looking forward to it. Should I bring anything, like a cake or something?'

'No need. Not that there'll be anything too fancy. You already know Mum's cooking abilities.'

'She made a great meal the other night.'

'Yeah,' I said, with more than a touch of pride. 'But I wouldn't count on it happening again too soon. Anyway, I better go. I'm babysitting tonight so I need to get home early.'

'See you tomorrow then, Zoe.' He looked as if he was about to say something else, but then seemed to change his mind. He nodded and then was on his way.

# Chapter Fourteen

Dad had come good with his promise of getting a babysitting job for me. One of his workmates asked if I could look after his son. My parents had met him and his wife at a Christmas party for Dad's work and they said the Stewarts seemed nice. So I thought surely their kid would be okay. I was usually pretty good with kids, which was why I didn't mind babysitting for extra pocket money. I had a few tricks up my sleeve for dealing with kids that were cranky, bored or didn't want to go to bed. So, no probs.

Dad dropped me off at the Stewarts' inner-city house. A thin lady with blonde bobbed hair opened the door, and the sound of classical music drifted out.

'You must be Zoe,' she said, smiling. 'I'm so glad you could help us out. Our au pair, Giselle, has gone home to France for a holiday. Please, come in.'

I stepped into a white-walled hallway that had a fancy gilt-framed mirror on one side and a large black-and-orange abstract painting on the opposite wall near a stairway. Mrs Stewart led the way down the hallway to a room at the back, which was connected to a stainless-steel kitchen.

'This is our family room. It'll be more comfortable for you than the main lounge and dining areas. Please sit down, Zoe. I'll just go over a few things so you know the routine. Emerson is upstairs practising his flute.'

Alarm bells started to tinkle. I set great store by kids' names. Usually the fancier the name, the worse the kid was. But maybe I was judging too quickly, I decided. I should keep an open mind.

'Sure, Mrs Stewart,' I said, sitting on the black leather sofa and looking around. Where, I wondered, was the TV?

Mrs Stewart picked up a sheet of paper from the coffee table and handed it to me before sitting down in the armchair opposite me. 'This is Emerson's schedule.'

Schedule? I glanced down at the sheet, which seemed to have an awful lot of information for the few hours I was going to be here.

'Emerson,' Mrs Stewart said, fixing me with her pale blue eyes, 'is a highly strung, extremely intelligent child who needs constant stimulation if he's not to become bored.'

'I've had a lot of experience looking after children,' I said, trying to be reassuring, but whether it was for her benefit or my own I wasn't quite sure.

'So your father said. But our child is not like others. We have rather high expectations of him, and naturally we expect that anyone looking after him will reinforce those.'

I nodded, not knowing what else to say. Was it too late to back out of this job?

'So we expect you to adhere to this schedule, because any change in the routine could be upsetting for Emerson.'

'Yes, of course, children do like a routine.' That, at least, I knew. My little cousins, however, always managed to get around me and stay up a bit later than their regular bedtime. But flexibility and fun were important, too.

I looked down and read: *Converse in French, play chess, read stimulating book, practise yoga exercises, shower and bed.* There didn't seem much room for fun and flexibility there. There were also helpful hints for me, the 'care provider', such as: *Emerson does not respond well to a raised voice. Logic and reasoned discussion work best.*

Well, at least he would be in bed by eight-thirty, so then I could relax.

'My mobile number's at the top of that sheet, should you need to contact me. We should be home by eleven. Any questions, Zoe?' She raised pointed eyebrows.

'What does he have for a bedtime snack?'

A look of disapproval swept over her face. 'Oh, we don't believe in eating between meals. It's most upsetting for the digestion. And Emerson has several allergies, so we have to be very careful of his diet. He may have some filtered water if he's thirsty, but he had his dinner half an hour ago so he shouldn't need anything until the morning. Do you play chess, by the way?'

I shook my head.

She sighed, giving me the feeling that I was lacking in my babysitting abilities.

I felt the need to say, 'I do play checkers and Scrabble.'

'Checkers is rather elementary for Emerson. He would be so bored. I suppose you could play Scrabble, as long as it's in French.'

'I'm afraid I don't know French,' I said, feeling like the biggest failure ever.

I could see her trying to hide her disappointment in me, which made it worse. 'Then perhaps you could play it in English, but do stipulate that there's to be no one-syllable words. He must have some challenge.'

'How old is Emerson?' I expected her to say ten or eleven, at least.

'Six,' she said, rising gracefully from her chair.

I tried to keep my jaw from dropping. Who was this genius I was about to look after?

She looked at her watch. 'He should be finished practice by now. I'll go and get him.'

I looked around the barren room, where I was to spend the next few hours with a six year old. Sofa, two armchairs, coffee table and bookcase, and paintings in gilt frames. Everything was pin neat. Surely there would be a TV somewhere in this house if he got bored. Maybe there was one in his bedroom, which had to be more child-friendly than this room. Anyway, Emerson would know.

And no food? I always looked forward to the snacks people usually left for their children and the babysitter. Popcorn, cola, maybe even a slice or two of pizza. I was wishing I'd brought a chocolate bar or something. Even Mum's slightly burnt brownies were starting to look good.

Mrs Stewart came back with Emerson. He looked exactly as I had pictured him. He was short and skinny, with neat blond hair and blue eyes, a clone of his mother. He wore a short-sleeved shirt with a collar and a perfectly pressed pair of navy shorts. Instead of sneakers or thongs, he had on a pair of buckled sandals, which looked like what a kid from the royal family would wear.

'Emerson, this is Zoe. She'll be looking after you tonight.'

'Hi, Emerson,' I said, giving him my best child-friendly smile.

He gave me a piercing look, not unlike his mother's, and held out a hand to me, saying, '*Bonjour*, Zoe. *Comment-allez vous?*'

As I shook his hand, his mother gave a superior little laugh and said, 'Oh no, dear, Zoe doesn't speak French like Giselle.'

He looked at her in surprise. 'Then how am I to practise my French tonight, Mummy?'

'I'm sorry, but you'll have to read one of your French storybooks, or the basic French grammar one, if you want to revise. We'll have to make do tonight.'

At that moment I heard footsteps in the hall, and a voice called, 'Are you ready, Rebecca? We've got to get going. You know what the traffic's like this time of night.'

A tall, redheaded guy in a suit burst in the door. He looked at me and smiled. 'You must be Zoe. Thanks for coming over at such short notice.'

'No worries,' I said, feeling relief. He, at least, looked and sounded normal.

'I've been ready for at least quarter of an hour,' Mrs Stewart said, smoothing the non-existent wrinkles from her black dress. 'I've just been going over a few things with Zoe.' She reached up and straightened his tie. 'I do think the blue one would've gone better with this suit.'

He shrugged. 'Haven't time to change it now. We don't want to be late.'

'No, of course not, I wouldn't dream of making Eloise and Jonathan wait for us. Kiss Mummy goodbye,' she said, turning to Emerson. He gave a peck on the cheek she presented to him.

'Okay, we'll be off then, Zoe,' Mr Stewart said. 'I believe Rebecca gave you our number if there's any problem. We won't be too late. And Emerson, be good.' He ruffled his son's hair and headed out the door again.

Mrs Stewart turned before leaving, and said, 'Emerson is always good. Aren't you, my dear?' She smoothed his hair down again.

'Of course, Mummy,' he said, in a perfectly angelic voice.

She left, leaving a trail of expensive perfume behind her.

I heard the front door close. Alone at last. I let out the breath that I didn't realise I was holding.

Turning to Emerson, I said, 'Well, Emerson, what would you like to do?'

He looked at me with calculating eyes. 'I have a schedule, you know.'

'Oh yes, of course.' I looked down at the printed sheet. 'So it looks like French, first up. Where are your books?'

'You don't speak French and I don't want to read. We can play chess instead.'

'How about Scrabble?'

'That's for babies.' He lifted his eyebrows in a perfect imitation of his mother.

'I don't know how to play chess, but I could learn, I guess. You could teach me.' I spoke hopefully. After all, if a six year old could learn I was sure I could.

'You don't speak French and you don't play chess. Just why did my mother hire you? Giselle could speak three languages.' He looked at me accusingly. 'And if I have to teach you, I'm the one who should get paid, not you.'

'I'm a babysitter, not a teacher,' I said, speaking firmly.

He put his hands on his waist. 'I'm not a *baby*. And now I'm bored. It's not good for me to be bored. I need stimulation.'

'Well, Scrabble is fun, too. You can use long words. I'm sure you must know several.'

He gave me a look of distain. 'I have a reading age of fifteen-plus and a superior IQ. My mother had me tested.'

Of course she did, I thought. 'Well, let's try out that skill, then. Where's the Scrabble?'

'I don't think you'll be much of a challenge,' he said, but opened the deep drawer in the coffee table and took out a couple of games. There was chess, Scrabble and a pack of cards.

'Oh, cards, I know a couple of card games.'

'I'm learning to play bridge, but we haven't enough people for that.'

I didn't tell him that I didn't know how to play bridge, either.

We played Scrabble for about ten minutes and in no time he was beating me.

After a few more minutes, this mini-genius sat back on his small bottom and said, 'I've had enough. This is not stimulating. I need stimulation. Amuse me.'

'Pardon?'

'Amuse me. That's your job, isn't it?'

'We could watch some TV or a DVD, maybe.' I could clearly see this schedule thing wasn't going to work.

'I never watch TV. Mummy doesn't allow it. She says it would weaken my brain.'

'Well, then, I could read you a story.'

'I'm perfectly capable of reading to myself.' He got up and wandered towards the kitchen. 'I'm hungry. I want a snack.'

'Your mother said you're not to eat before bedtime.' And how I wished that time was now.

'I'm bored. When I get bored I get hungry. I want something to eat *now*.' His reedy little voice rose.

'I'm sorry, Emerson, I have to follow your mother's instructions. And so do you.' I didn't like this child, but I was starting to feel sorry for him, just a little.

'You mustn't say no to me. I don't like it. I'm highly strung, you know.' He glared at me.

'I'll get you some water, and then maybe we can go upstairs to your bedroom and play with some of your toys.'

I went into the ultra-tidy kitchen and opened the fridge to take out the water jug.

'I don't want water. I want something to eat. And I don't play with toys. They're for babies.'

I put the jug on the kitchen counter. 'Maybe a piece of fruit, then.' Surely his mother couldn't object to that. I'd seen some apples and grapes in the fridge.

He folded his arms. 'I don't want fruit.'

'Perhaps I could make you a nice sandwich. There must be some peanut butter in one of the cupboards.'

'Yuck. I don't eat that. I have a nut allergy. Do you want me to get sick?'

'No, no, of course not,' I said. 'Well, what can you eat?' I was getting desperate. Why had I taken this job?

'I want some lactose-free Italian gelato. Mummy keeps some in the freezer for dinner parties.'

'I don't think we should be using that if it's for special occasions.' It was time to use my firm but fair voice. 'You can have an apple or some grapes. That's it.' I stared him down.

'I want some gelato.'

'Let's go and play some more Scrabble. Or I have a few card tricks I can show you.'

'No. I want some gelato *now*.' His voice rose.

So much for logic and reasoned discussion.

'You heard what I said.' I didn't raise my voice, not even a little.

'*Give me some gelato now!*' he shouted.

I retreated from the kitchen to the family room, grabbed a magazine (*Home Beautiful*, of course) from the coffee table and pretended to read. I'd found in the past that ignoring temper tantrums was the best strategy.

And Emerson had a doozy.

He screamed and screamed. I turned a page, not looking up. He threw himself on the floor, and kicked and screamed some more. I stifled a yawn and stretched out my feet, but I could feel my nerves straining and my resolve weakening.

Then he got up, took the water jug and smashed it on the floor. It was glass—no one like Mrs Stewart would use something as cheap or practical as plastic—and it shattered on the tiles in about a million pieces.

Now, I'm a patient person with kids. I'm great at distracting normal kids and making them laugh. We sometimes even have fun together. But this kid was the most obnoxious child I'd ever met.

I dropped the magazine. He stood in the middle of the chaos with a triumphant look on his face. He had, thankfully, stopped screaming.

'I thought that would get your attention,' he said calmly. 'Now, you may get me my gelato.'

With glass all over the place, I was in no mood to argue with him. I carefully manoeuvred around the shards, picked him up and plonked him on the sofa.

'Stay there and don't move,' I said, in a voice that sounded eerily like my mother's when she was angry. 'Otherwise I'll be calling your *mummy* right now to tell her how naughty you've been.'

'You won't,' he said, 'because then I'll tell her it was all your fault, and that *you* broke the jug. I'll also tell her you didn't follow the schedule.'

I ignored him and went to the kitchen to clean up the mess he'd made. I didn't notice until I was nearly finished that it was very quiet. Not a good sign. I finished sweeping up the glass and put the pieces in the bin. I looked for Emerson in the family room but he wasn't there.

I went down the hallway, calling out to him. I looked into the lounge, where brocaded chairs and a white grand piano filled the room. Jeez, cosy much. No sign of Emerson.

I called out again and looked up the stairs. Maybe he'd gone to his room.

Upstairs, I passed the main bedroom and found a smaller room, which I thought was a guest room at first. It had paintings and a vase of flowers next to a large queen-size bed that had a white quilt cover. Then I saw a music stand and a flute case next to it. A small pair of slippers was next to the bed.

Surely this bare, uninviting room couldn't be Emerson's? And there was no one in it. I was beginning to panic as I checked the bathroom and toilets.

'Emerson, where are you? Come out and I'll get you some gelato.'

No answer. I raced downstairs again, looking in cupboards and anywhere I could think of. There was a door in the hallway that I thought must lead to the garage. Opening it, I went inside and there he was. My heart went up into my mouth.

He was balancing on a box on a chair next to a metal shelf filled with tins of paint and tools. The chair had wheels, and I knew that any little movement could send the box and Emerson toppling.

He reached up and pulled a small plastic bag from between some tins. 'I knew it was there,' he said, in a small but triumphant voice.

I went over to him and said quietly, 'Emerson, you need to come down from there before you fall.'

He turned around and the chair moved. The box wobbled, the chair moved again and he fell, straight into my arms. We both toppled to the hard concrete floor, him on top of me. Thank goodness I had cushioned the fall for him. He didn't seem hurt. The fact that I did, in several places, didn't seem important at the moment.

He burst into tears and put his arms around my neck. 'I want Giselle,' he sobbed.

I sat us both up and held him close, letting him cry. He'd been a horrible kid, but right now he was just a normal little guy crying for someone he missed. And I couldn't help noticing that he wasn't crying for his mother.

'It's okay,' I said, 'you'll be fine.'

His tears subsided to some loud sniffs.

'Why don't we get you some gelato?' I said. The hell with the rules, I thought.

He looked at me and gave a sunny smile, which made him look like he was actually six. 'No need, I found Dad's secret stash.' He held up a plastic bag and then opened it, showing me the Cherry Ripe, Snickers and Mars bars inside. 'He hides it in here so Mummy doesn't know.'

I didn't know what to say.

'You can have one if you want.'

'I'm not sure we should be taking anything that belongs to your dad.'

He shrugged his shoulders. 'He won't mind. He shares with me sometimes. It's our little secret.' He gave me a wink.

I know I should have said no. And if it had happened an hour earlier I probably would have. But I was really starting to feel sorry for this kid, with every minute of his day timetabled and not even one toy in his room.

'Come on,' he said, putting his hand in mine. 'I'll be good now.'

I sighed. 'Okay, well, just one. And you better have some milk or something to go with it.'

'Can't,' he said. 'I'm lactose intolerant.'

We went back into the main house and I taught him how to play Snap, which he loved, and we ate chocolate. Then he had his shower, put on his pyjamas and got into that big white bed.

'I can read you a story, if you want. I know you can read, but I do really good voices.'

'Giselle reads to me sometimes. I miss her,' he said, with a sigh.

'I know, matey, but I'll do my best.'

To my surprise, he snuggled into me and I put my arm around him.

He looked up at me and said, 'It's hard to be so smart. I'm different from everyone else and no one wants to be my friend at school. It isn't much fun.'

A name popped into my head. 'I know someone who's really smart, and he's very nice, too.'

'As smart as me?'

'Smarter. He knows all about science and he's learning Mandarin Chinese. In fact, he knows more than the teachers at my school.'

'What's his name?'

'Rion. It's short for Orion, which is the name of a constellation.'

'Can he play chess?'

'He's an expert. He plays people online from all over the world.' How did I know that? I didn't. And yet I did.

'But I bet he doesn't have fun.' Emerson's eyes were getting droopy.

I stopped and thought for a moment. Then I said, 'Yes, he does. He also watches TV and he even goes bowling. Sometimes he eats junk food, too. You can be smart, Emerson, and still do fun things. And being different is okay, you know.'

'I'd like to meet him sometime.' Emerson closed his eyes.

'Maybe you will,' I said. 'You'd really like him.' But Emerson was fast asleep.

I moved away from him gently and covered him over. He wasn't such a bad little kid, after all.

As I crept out of his room and went downstairs, I thought about what I'd told Emerson. How did I know all that stuff about Rion? In some ways Emerson reminded me of Rion. Emerson was smart and he knew a lot, but he didn't know how to be a kid. Just like Rion hadn't known how to be … human?

I shook my head. That was a crazy thought.

Obviously this night had rattled my brain as well as my nerves. Rion was just some guy who had stayed with us for a couple of months. I cleaned up the chocolate wrappers and put the remaining loot back in the garage where

Emerson had found it. I was beginning to understand the need for secrecy where Rebecca Stewart was concerned. Then I reluctantly took out my books and started on my maths homework. That, if anything, was sure to bring me back to reality.

That night, when I finally got home, I looked out my window and saw the Orion constellation. Somehow, I felt a connection to it. It had a meaning for me, but I just didn't know what it was.

# Chapter Fifteen

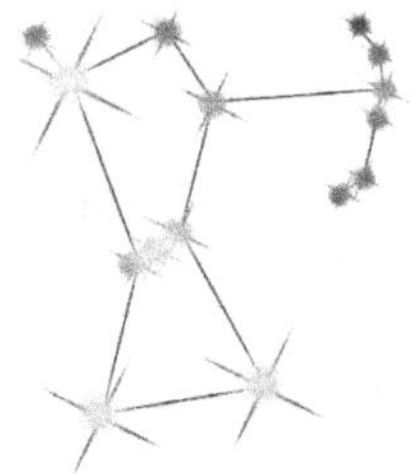

I wasn't nervous. Not really. Well, maybe a little. I'd bought some chocolates for Zoe's mother. After that disastrous dinner a few weeks ago, I felt I'd better do something. I was surprised they even wanted to see me again. One thing was clear: I was never going to let them or anyone else meet Archimedes again. He was a definite liability.

So, there was no reason to get worried or nervous. No reason at all, I thought, as I ironed a perfect crease in my school trousers and then repolished my black shoes. At least Archimedes had done one thing right. We'd both had a variety of interesting facts to tell the Brennans about the Amazon rainforest. I thought that had gone well, although they hadn't seemed as impressed as I'd hoped they'd be.

The school day seemed to be much longer than the six hours and twenty-six minutes it actually was. I didn't see much of Zoe, except in class, because at lunchtime I had my job helping out in the school lab. I was pleased when Mr Hasan, the chemistry teacher, offered it to me again.

After school on Wednesday, I waited at the school gate for Zoe. I had no idea why my pulse quickened or my temperature rose when I saw her coming towards me, her dark hair swinging and her mouth curved up in a smile. I was grateful the blemish on my chin was barely noticeable.

'Hey,' she said, stopping beside me.

We swung into step together, heading towards her house. It was a walk we had done so many times before and I wondered if it wakened a memory inside her.

'How was your day?' I asked, not perhaps the most brilliant of conversation starters, especially since we were in a few classes together.

She shrugged. 'Same old, same old. If I hear about how important this senior year is one more time from the teachers, I'm going to scream. Like, I get it. I don't need to hear it a hundred times.'

'But you'll be fine. After all, you did well last year, didn't you?' I'd been impressed when she'd told me her results. When I first met her, Zoe wasn't exactly the most studious of people.

'Only because I had no life,' she said. 'Anyway, you don't need to worry. You'll probably be dux of the school. What are you going to do next year?'

Her question caught me off guard. I really had no plans at all, other than to blend in and not look out of place. And maybe get Zoe to like me again. 'I don't know. I haven't decided yet. What about you?'

'Same. I'm still trying to decide, too. But I'm trying to do better in science, not my area of strength. But if I manage not to totally flunk it, that won't go against me at the end of the year.'

'I could help you.' I looked at her and smiled. At least it would give me an excuse to spend more time with her.

'Maybe,' she said. 'You did help me understand that chemistry homework. I also seem to remember you were pretty good at helping with physics, at least that was what Jas said last year.' She looked at me with just the hint of a smile on her face.

I felt like cringing. I remembered only too well how that had ended. Jas had given me my first kiss ever. But it hadn't been my last one or my best. I looked at Zoe, wondering if she remembered. I tried not to think about the recent kiss Jas had given me, which, as far as I was concerned, didn't count.

But she seemed not to, since all she did was laugh.

We were quiet for a while, and then she said, 'I had the worst babysitting job ever last night, with the weirdest little kid.'

'I'm sure you handled him all right.' Zoe was good with people, far better than I'd ever be.

'Not at first,' she said. 'He was supposed to be, like, this super-genius. But he was horrible, at least at first.'

She told me about her night, and I was impressed by the way she had handled the situation so calmly. And of course the child had been won over by her in the end.

'So you actually let him have that chocolate. I wouldn't have, and he'd probably still have been screaming when his parents got home.'

'But you wouldn't have been in that situation to start with.'

'Why not?' I was puzzled.

'Because you're super-smart and you'd have beaten him at chess. Even his mother would've been impressed with you.'

'But I don't speak French.'

'You speak Chinese and you could've amazed them with that.'

'I have the fundamentals of Mandarin Chinese, although I'm by no means bilingual.'

'You see? That's what I mean. There's no way a sentence like that could come from a normal sixteen-year-old guy.'

'Seventeen,' I said, remembering that now I was human, my body was ageing normally.

'Whatever. I told Emerson about you. I said you were really smart and still managed to have fun. Poor kid, I don't think his mother's ever let him do anything remotely like fun. He said he'd like to meet you.'

'I don't have a problem with that. I'd like to see just how good his chess is. I've been needing a challenge lately.'

Zoe rolled her eyes. 'OMG, his mother would just love you.'

I shrugged. 'I don't think the feeling would be mutual. She doesn't sound like a very nurturing sort of person. Even on my planet, a certain degree of parental affection is considered important.'

'What?'

I nearly clapped my hand over my mouth, but it was too late anyway. How had I forgotten myself to the extent that I could say something like that?

Zoe was looking at me with an incredulous look on her face. 'What did you just say?' She stopped in her tracks and whirled around to face me.

'Nothing, it was a joke, that's all.' I attempted a lame smile.

'Weird joke,' she said, tilting her head to one side and giving me an intense stare.

'I'm not very good at jokes.'

'So I seem to remember,' she said, with a thoughtful look on her face.

We started to walk again and I was relieved to see that it wasn't too much further to her house. The less time I had to say or do something stupid, the better.

'Anyway, your mum left you to go to Cairns with her boyfriend. I don't think that was very caring—' She stopped walking abruptly. 'I'm sorry. I shouldn't have said that.' She was looking at me and biting her lip.

Last year Zoe and I had concocted a story to explain my sudden presence to her parents. Obviously Zoe had forgotten that it was a fabrication and thought it was real. But it was better to have her think she'd hurt my feelings than to remember the truth.

I shrugged. 'That's okay, you're right. She wasn't very caring.'

We were both quiet until we reached her home. Perhaps we'd both said things we shouldn't. I knew I'd have to be more careful from now on.

Mrs Brennan was already home from her teaching job. She gave me a hug. I remembered the way Zoe's mum had always made me feel so welcome. I gave her the chocolates, which I hoped hadn't melted in my locker.

'That's thoughtful of you,' she said, 'thank you. I'm so glad you could come to dinner, Rion. We never really had a chance to catch up properly last time. Not that we didn't enjoy meeting your uncle. He's such an interesting man.'

Mrs Brennan was just as diplomatic as her daughter.

'Thanks for inviting me. Can I help with anything?'

'No, it's all in hand. Just don't expect anything as fancy as beef Wellington. I thought I'd better play it safe tonight. Can't expect two miracles in a row.' She smiled at me.

'I've always liked your cooking, Mrs Brennan,'

'What a suck-up,' Zoe said, and laughed.

I was about to protest when she grabbed me by the hand and pulled me out of the kitchen.

'Come on,' she said. 'If you want to be helpful, you can help me with chemistry again. Boring, I know, but you did offer and it'd be good to get it out of the way 'cause it's due tomorrow.'

'But we got that assignment on Monday. I thought you'd have done it by now,' I said, as we went upstairs. This felt very familiar.

'Seriously? Don't you know me by now? I might've improved my grades, but I haven't had a total personality transplant.'

I stopped at the door to her room. It was utter chaos. The bed was unmade and clothes were strewn across the floor. Archimedes would have had a very human heart attack if I'd left my room like that.

'Oops, I think we'll go into the spare room, where you used to be. It's less cluttered.' She pushed me towards the room that held so many memories for me.

'Good choice, I see you're just as untidy as ever,' was my accurate but not entirely wise reply.

'And I can see you're just as anal,' she said.

It was like déjà vu. We'd had so many conversations like this in the past, but I decided not to mention that fact so I must have learnt something these past few months.

Instead, I said, 'Sorry, I can be too truthful at times.'

She sat down on the bed. 'And that's supposed to make it better? Never mind. You did me a favour. I'd almost forgotten why you annoyed me last year.' She gave me a smile to soften her words. 'Just as well you make up for it by being smart.'

I took a deep breath. I was surprised at how much that remark affected me. She still didn't remember that at one time she had liked me, at least a little.

'So, about this homework,' she said, as she opened her chemistry book, 'I don't suppose you could just give me the answers. It'd save a lot of time.'

'But you wouldn't learn anything that way. It would be much better if I explained things first and then you worked out the answers—'

I stopped as she broke out in laughter.

'Chill, Rion, I was only stirring you. I actually do want to get more than a pass in chemistry this year. Jeez, you and Kerri have a lot in common.'

'At least I'm helping you,' I said.

'True. She wouldn't even do that.'

It was strange to be in such a familiar situation and yet have so many conflicting feelings. Being back in my old room made me feel as if nothing had changed. And it was so much more comfortable than my sterile room in the townhouse. That place had no atmosphere, no sense of home.

Yet everything was different now. Zoe had no memories of who I really was, or our special connection, which had always helped when we had small clashes, like now. I missed our closeness.

When we went down to dinner, Zoe's dad was there. 'Good to see you again, Rion, almost like old times again, eh?'

It felt good being with the Brennans again, although they still wanted to know more about my experiences in the Brazilian rainforest. Apparently, facts weren't enough.

'But what was it *really* like, Rion?' Zoe's mum asked. 'Where did you stay? Who did you meet? What were your impressions? It's such a fascinating place, and you must have had some memorable experiences.'

I hesitated for a moment, conscious of the fact that all three pairs of eyes were on me. Impressions? Experiences? How could I talk intelligently about the Amazon when I'd never been there? I searched for something to say. 'Um, yes, it was very interesting, very memorable.'

'And?' Mrs Brennan's brown eyes, so much like Zoe's, were looking at me.

I reviewed my encyclopaedic memory to see what I could come up with. 'The indigenous people of the rainforest are very friendly and surprisingly non-materialistic, although their living conditions are almost primitive compared to Western standards.'

'So, who did you meet?' Mrs Brennan persisted.

I'd always found it difficult to lie, and now more than ever. I respected the Brennan family and didn't want to say anything to them that wasn't true. I had in the past, but only out of necessity.

'Various people from different tribes,' I said. 'One of the head tribesmen was very kind to me. He told me the native remedies for relieving mosquito bite.'

'Where did you sleep?' Zoe asked.

I knew the answer 'various places' wouldn't do. 'In huts, you know, with the people. They were very hospitable.'

'It must've been damn uncomfortable at times,' Zoe's dad said, 'especially for your uncle.'

Mrs Brennan nudged him.

'Yes it was, but we managed.'

'So, tell us about when you saw the anacondas,' Zoe said.

'The snakes? That was very interesting. Did you know that the longest anaconda recorded was 7.6 metres in length.'

'How big was the one you saw, and where did you see it?' she asked.

'Um, about four metres, so it was probably a female. We saw it swimming in the river.' I was mixing fact with fiction so fast that I was bound to trip up. I should never have agreed to come for dinner.

'Did you get photos?' she asked eagerly.

I gave the only excuse I could come up with. 'No, my phone went flat.'

'But your uncle's a photojournalist. Surely he carried a camera.' Mrs Brennan looked surprised.

'He wasn't with me that time. He was back at camp, resting.' I really wished they would change the subject.

Mr Brennan raised a brow and said softly, 'That figures.'

He received another nudge from Mrs Brennan, who said, 'I hope he didn't leave you on your own too often, especially in such a dangerous environment.'

I squirmed, not knowing how to answer this. 'Archimedes is a most suitable guardian who looks after me well.' And that was the biggest lie I had told all evening.

Mr Brennan shot me a sharp look and turned to his wife. 'Where's that dessert you promised us, dear? The kids have school tomorrow so we don't want too late a night.'

'Oh yes, of course. I hope you don't mind, but it's not homemade. Just ice cream and some fresh fruit.'

'That sounds great, Mum,' Zoe said, jumping up. 'Why don't you sit down and I'll get it.'

'I'll help,' I said, anything to avoid the cross-examination of my non-existent trip to the Amazon rainforest.

In the kitchen, Zoe took the ice cream from the freezer and turned to me. 'Rion, what really happened on that Amazon trip?'

I opened the fridge, making sure she couldn't see my face. 'What you mean? Where's the fruit salad?'

'In the Tupperware container with the blue lid, and you know what I mean. You might be able to trick Mum and Dad, but not me. I know you too well for that.'

I found the container and put it on the kitchen counter, still not willing to face her. But Zoe put a hand on my arm and turned me around. I was forced to look into her too-knowing brown eyes.

In my defence, I said, 'You surprise me, Zoe, I was under the impression you hardly remembered anything about me; that my time with your family meant nothing to you.'

I immediately realised I shouldn't have said that. It wasn't Zoe's fault that she couldn't remember; it was mine. Perhaps I was hoping our connection was strong enough that she would at least remember liking me. But I knew it was irrational to think that. Archimedes had said he would also take away Zoe's memory of her feelings for me.

That was what I wanted. And yet it wasn't. I had never been so confused in all my previous four thousand years of existence.

It was too dangerous an area to delve into. After all, I was the one who hadn't wanted Zoe to remember exactly who I was or what our connection had been.

For a moment her eyes flickered and I sensed her uncertainty, and also, strangely, I could see the hurt. Then she said, 'I don't exactly remember everything, that's true. But I do feel that I know you better than I thought. We shared something, Rion. I just can't remember what. And whenever I try, my mind seems all foggy and confused.'

We looked at each other, and just for a second, maybe even a nanosecond, there was something there, a connection. Our breaths seemed to synchronise, and I could feel the beat of her heart as it kept time with mine. I lifted a hand to touch her cheek … and a car backfired outside.

She jumped, and my hand fell back to my side. The moment was over. We retreated into ourselves once more.

'But I do know you haven't been telling the whole truth about your trip to the Amazon,' Zoe said, moving away from me. 'All you can give is facts and figures. You haven't said one real thing that would prove you were actually there. What's going on?'

I knew I should lie to her again, because that would be best for both of us. But I couldn't do it any longer. I couldn't tell her the whole truth either, not yet and not here. I knew that soon I would have to make another decision. Perhaps I would ask Archimedes to restore her memories.

'It's complicated. You have to trust me on this, Zoe. I can't tell you everything at the moment. Don't worry, I haven't been in trouble or done anything wrong,' I added hastily as I saw her face cloud over.

'Did anything … bad happen? Archimedes isn't unkind to you or anything.'

I saw the anxious look on her face and said, 'No, no, of course not. He means well, even if he is a little strange.'

'Is he even your uncle? You're nothing like him.'

I hesitated a moment and then said, 'Technically, no. But he is my guardian.'

'Oh,' she said, and looked thoughtful. 'You know you can trust me, Rion. Whatever it is, I wouldn't tell anybody.'

I wanted to tell her the truth so badly. But that would have been selfish and only complicate matters even more. 'I know that, Zoe. I trust you more than anyone I know. I care about you and I'd never do anything to hurt you. I'm your friend. But now is not the best time.'

'I see.' She turned from me and started to serve the ice cream into the bowls she'd set out. 'Put the kettle on for tea and coffee, will you?'

I did as she asked, waiting for her to say something more. But she was quiet until she had the bowls ready to take into the dining room. Then she turned to me.

'You said you didn't want to hurt me. Too late, Rion, especially since you don't trust me enough to tell me the truth. And friends, *real* friends, don't lie to each other.' Then she turned her back on me and left the kitchen.

Nobody brought up the Amazon trip again. Mr and Mrs Brennan talked about other things and we even shared a laugh or two. Zoe remained quiet. When we finished the meal, I offered to help with the washing up, but Zoe's mum wouldn't let me.

'Not necessary,' she said, 'but thanks, Rion. It was just lovely having you here again.'

I thanked her and got ready to leave. I didn't want to prolong this evening any more than necessary, considering what Zoe had said. I couldn't see how I could make things better, or explain. Perhaps it was best that I didn't try. At least not right then, not with her parents there.

Mr Brennan insisted on driving me home, even though I said I could walk.

'You go on with Dad,' Zoe said. 'I'll stay home. I'm a bit tired and I have an exam tomorrow.'

I wasn't surprised.

So Mr B drove me the short distance to that empty townhouse that I now called home.

'It was great to see you tonight, Rion. Don't be a stranger,' he said, as I got out.

I found his words ironic because that's exactly what Zoe and I had become, strangers. And it seemed the more we had to do with each other, the truer that was.

# Chapter Sixteen

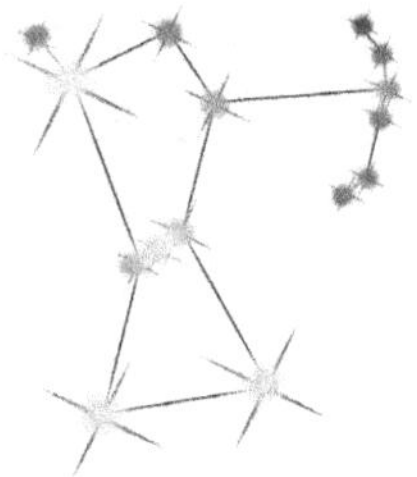

'I'm super-excited about the play on Thursday,' Lou said, taking the lid off her salad container. 'It's going to be so much fun.'

'I don't know about that, Lou,' I said, 'but at least everyone's going now that Jas has managed to wind Ms D around her little finger.' Jas had perfected the art of manipulation, but I wasn't going to complain about a day off.

'What are you going to wear, Zoe?'

I wasn't exactly a fashion guru, but considering the only other female in our group was Keri, whose idea of dressing up was a clean T-shirt, I understood why Lou asked me.

'I don't know. I haven't thought about it.' My wardrobe wasn't all that extensive, so my choices would be limited.

'I wish they'd make us all wear our school uniforms. That would be so much easier,' Kerri said.

I almost agreed with her. Everyone (well, the girls at least) would be trying to outdo each other. But we might as well give up before we started because we all knew who would look the most fabulous. Jas had a wardrobe that would rival the Myers Miss Shop.

'Why don't you come over to my place this afternoon, Zoe?' Lou said, with hopeful eyes. 'We can decide together.'

I hesitated a moment. I liked Lou, but we weren't exactly at the braiding-hair-and-sleepover stage. I hadn't had a close girl pal since my best friend, Mandy, went to Sydney last year. But I knew that saying no without a good reason would probably hurt Lou, so I shrugged and said, 'Sure.'

'Great, I'll meet you after school.' Lou beamed.

'I haven't got time to waste on stuff like that,' Kerri said with a frown. 'I have a ton of homework to do.' She was totally oblivious to the fact that she hadn't been invited.

'Of course, Kerri, I understand,' Lou said diplomatically.

Harry came sauntering over the grass and sat down beside me. 'Hey, guys.'

'We were just talking about the play on Thursday,' Lou said.

'I wouldn't go at all if we weren't getting Friday off,' Kerri said. 'At least it'll give me the whole day to study.'

Harry smiled at her. 'You could get an A standing on your head, Kerri. Why don't you take the day off? Go to the beach or something.'

She turned her shocked face towards him. 'Are you serious? You do realise we have a maths exam next week, not to mention we have to write a report on the play. A day off to study is like gold. I have so much to do as it is.'

And none of it fun, I thought.

'Chill, Kerri, I'm only teasing you,' Harry said.

'You have a strange sense of humour.' Kerri took a comforting bite of her chicken-and-salad wrap, which she had every day because it saved time thinking about what to eat and, as she'd told us many times, it had the perfect balance of fibre, protein, vitamins and minerals.

Just then, Rion came out of the school building and headed towards us. He must have finished his job in the lab early. Almost without realising it, I moved a couple of centimetres away from Harry.

Mine were not the only eyes that rested on Rion as he strolled towards us with that slight swagger and confident air that he didn't even realise he had. His dark hair skimmed his even darker eyes, which looked at you as if he knew exactly what you were thinking. And when he smiled, it was, I have to admit, knee weakening.

Which was kind of annoying, especially since I knew he was keeping something from me. So much for us being friends. Still, it wasn't exactly a newsflash that nearly every girl in senior year noticed him, and would have jumped at the chance to go out with him.

Except me, of course. And Keri. I'd noticed that even Lou had given Rion an interested look once or twice. Not that he'd noticed.

He sat down on the other side of me. I concentrated on eating my apple and ignoring him. But I was worried. What was he hiding from me? And maybe it wasn't entirely his fault. I wasn't sure how much I trusted Archimedes.

It was nearly the end of lunchtime when Jas walked over to us. The sun glinted on the blonde highlights in her hair and her cool blue eyes had a sense of purpose in them. I wondered what was up. Jas coming over to our group couldn't possibly mean anything good.

Ignoring us, she zeroed in on Rion. 'Hey, Rion, about the play on Thursday, I can drive you. I'm not going on the bus, too crowded.' She shuddered. 'So I'm taking my car.'

'I thought we all had to go together on the bus,' Keri said, looking up from her book.

Jas gave her a look that would have wilted anyone else, but Kerri was unmoved. She just slid her glasses up her nose and looked at Jas as if she were examining something under a microscope.

'Mum called Ms D and got permission,' Jas said icily. Jas's mum was on the P&C and was one of the parents with influence in the school. Of course. She turned back to Rion, confident of his answer.

'What about Chad?' Rion asked. 'Shouldn't you be going with him?'

She shrugged. 'He's got football training and isn't going to the play.'

No surprises there, I thought. Chad would choose football over Shakespeare any day, even if it did mean having Friday off. But jeez, talk about a loyal girlfriend.

All eyes in our group turned to focus on Rion, wondering what he would say.

'Thanks, but I'll get the bus with the rest of the class,' he said.

Like a synchronised swimming team, our heads moved as one as we looked back at Jas. It was as good as a play—probably better than the one we were going to see.

She gave a sweet smile, which didn't quite make it to her eyes. 'I thought I was your friend, too, Rion. Especially after we had coffee that day in the valley. Don't tell me you've forgotten that.'

*Whoosh*. Our attention and collective gaze was back on Rion. Just what went on, I wondered, when they had coffee?

Rion looked confused and definitely embarrassed. 'Um, yes, of course I remember.'

'Good, because I really need to talk to you, but somewhere more private.' She sent a blazing look at everyone in our group and our eyes dropped to whatever was in our laps, lunch, books, hands, whatever. 'After school, today, I'll meet you at the gate.' She turned on her heel, walking away from us before he had a chance to say no.

Rion looked as if he'd been hit by a truck. I almost felt sorry for him.

'What do you think of this one?' Lou whisked out a fuchsia-pink dress that would look super-cute if you were six years old. 'I wore it to my sister's wedding.' She gave me a bright smile.

'Well … I'm sure it was great for the wedding, but it might be a bit formal for going to a play.'

'Ms D did say it was evening wear,' Lou said, as she reluctantly put the dress back in the wardrobe.

I was sitting on her bed surrounded by a rainbow of pastels, and a sea of flouncy skirts, bows and frills. 'Black is sometimes a good colour for evening,' I said.

'Mum says I'm too young for black.' She sighed, flopping down next to me. 'I'll never find anything to wear.'

'Sure you will,' I said, getting up to look in her wardrobe again. There wasn't much in it now, most of it being spread out on her bed and the chair in the corner. I slid the hangers across the bar methodically, concentrating on the task of find something that wouldn't make Lou look as if she were still in middle school.

'What about this?' I said, taking out a sea-blue dress with spaghetti straps. It wasn't perfect, but there wasn't a bow or frill in sight.

'Isn't that more of a sundress, like you'd wear shopping or something? I hardly ever wear it because it shows my bra straps and I haven't got a strapless bra.'

'You could wear it with this,' I said, taking out a darker blue bolero with silver sparkles. 'It'll cover your shoulders and dress it up a bit.'

'You think so?' Lou sounded doubtful.

'Yeah, try it on and see.'

Maybe I was a fashion guru after all, because the two together looked just right and the blues brought out the colour of Lou's eyes. Her light brown hair, out of its ponytail, skimmed her shoulders.

'You look really pretty, Lou,' I said, and meant it.

She twirled in front of the mirror and turned to me. 'Gee, I would never have thought of putting these two things together. Thanks, Zoe. I knew you'd be good at this.' She gave me a hug.

'Glad I could help,' I said.

After I'd helped her put back the clothes and was about to go home, she said, 'You should stay for dinner. Mum and Dad are going out tonight and it's just me. We can order pizza.'

'I don't know. It's a school night.' I don't think I'd ever used that excuse before in living memory.

Lou gave a dismissive wave of her hand. 'It's a short week, what with the play and Friday off. Anyway, you don't need to stay late. My parents will be home by nine and they can drive you home.'

I felt backed into a corner. I really didn't want to hurt her feelings. 'Sure,' I said.

Lou's mum was happy for me to stay. I think she was only too pleased to see that Lou had a friend around for a change.

'It'll be nice for Lou to have company. You should have some of your other friends around too sometime, Lou, like those nice girls you play tennis with. Do you play tennis, Zoe?'

I shook my head.

'You should try it. Great way to meet people, isn't it, darling?' She turned to Lou, who was starting to look embarrassed. 'Anyway, I'd better go and get ready. Your dad will be home any minute and we have a dinner reservation for six.'

As she disappeared, I said to Lou, 'I'd better call my parents and let them know.'

She nodded. 'I'll order the pizza.'

I didn't think it would be a problem staying, but when I called Mum, she said, 'Oh, that's a shame. Mrs Stewart called and wondered if you could babysit Emerson tonight. Something unexpected has turned up and she has to go out, but her husband's away for a few days on business. I know you didn't love going there, but they do pay well.'

They did indeed, and obviously Emerson hadn't dobbed me in for not following 'the schedule'. We'd gotten on okay at the end. And I could really do with the money for my driving lessons. Still, I knew Lou would be disappointed if I told her I couldn't stay. It was a big deal for her to have me there, and her mum would probably think it was Lou's fault and sign her up for yet another socially interactive sport—like golf or something.

'I kind of told Lou I would stay,' I told Mum.

'I understand and it is short notice. I think Rebecca Stewart believes the world revolves around her and her son. You don't know anyone else who could do it, do you?'

I was about to say no when a thought popped into my head. 'I could ask Rion.'

'That would be great. He's so responsible and kind. I'm sure Emerson would love him. Ask him, Zoe, and then tell him to call me if he agrees. He could probably do with some extra money.'

The more I thought about it the more I realised he would be the perfect babysitter for Emerson. They were both geeky and a little bit different. I was still upset with him for not telling me the whole truth about his Amazon trip, but I was worried about him, too. What was going on with him? Anyway, he could probably do with a break from Archimedes for one night.

He answered on the first ring. 'Zoe,' he said, and I could hear the surprise in his voice.

I decided to get straight to the point. 'Do you want a babysitting job tonight? I can't do it. It's Emerson, that kid I told you about. He's not easy, but the money's good.'

'Yes, I remember, and of course I'll do it. Emerson sounds interesting.'

'Yeah, *interesting*. That's what we said about Archimedes,' I said. 'Anyway, that's cool. Call Mum and let her know. She'll give you the details.'

I was about to go when he said, 'So what are you doing tonight that you can't babysit?'

'I'm having dinner at Lou's place.'

'Oh, Lou hey, that's nice.'

'Why did you ask?'

'No reason … I thought maybe you and Harry were going out.'

'No, but I'm surprised you're not busy with Jas. Didn't you meet with her after school?' I don't think I quite managed to keep the edge out of my voice.

'Yeah, but just briefly.' He sounded uncomfortable.

'So how'd that go?' I couldn't believe I was asking this question. I didn't even care, really.

He was quiet for a moment and then said, 'I'm not going with her to the play. I haven't changed my opinion about her. I should probably call your mother to get those details about the babysitting job.'

'Yeah, see you tomorrow.' I put the phone in the pocket of my school uniform. I wondered which opinion of Jas he meant. Was it the first one, when he told me last year that she was attractive and nice to him, or the second one, when he said he thought she was a bully and manipulative?

Boys, I knew, were so easily swayed when someone like Jas was involved. But he wasn't going with her to the play, so that was something.

I wandered out to the kitchen where Lou was preparing snacks. She had enough food on the kitchen table for an army rather than two sixteen-year-old girls. And there was still the pizza to come. But it was better than a whole lot of nothing to eat, which was what Rion would get when he went to the Stewarts' place

My meeting with Jas wasn't something I was eager to talk about, so I got off the phone with Zoe as quickly as I could. There was no way I wanted anyone to know what had happened between Jas and me this afternoon. Neither of us would come out looking good.

I'd met Jas after school, as she had commanded. But when she suggested we drive somewhere quiet for a talk, I gave her a definite no. I told her she could say what she wanted then and there, or not at all. So she did.

I knew that going out for coffee with Jas last week hadn't been a smart move, but I never realised it was a colossally stupid one. Jas gave me an ultimatum. Either I agreed to go to the play with her or she'd let everyone know I'd kissed her when we went for coffee.

'After all, you did come onto me. I mean, what was I to think? You led me on.'

'Jas, what are you doing? You have a boyfriend. You know there's nothing between us.'

For a moment it seemed like a mask had slipped from her face. All the confidence disappeared and I saw a vulnerable sixteen-year-old girl for a change.

'Rion, I really like you. I always have. Don't you like me, even a little?'

I didn't want to hurt her, but I had to be truthful. 'I'm sorry, Jas. It's not going to work. I just don't feel that way about you. You're a very attractive girl. If you don't want to be with Chad, you should tell him. I'm sure there'd be a long line of boys only too happy to take his place.'

The mask came on again and she snapped, 'I know that. I could have any guy I wanted. And by the way, you're lying. You didn't stop that kiss, Rion. In fact, you gave as good as you got. I wonder what your precious little Zoe would think about *that*.'

An unfamiliar surge of anger swept through me. I gave her a look that came straight from my soul, my four-thousand-year-old soul. 'You say or breath a word about that and I'll make sure Chad knows just what kind of girlfriend you really are.'

Her face paled and she took a step back from me. For a moment there was a deadly silence between us. Cars went past on the road, the school bus chugged by, and one or two students drifted out the school gate, too far away to have overheard anything of our heated discussion.

Then she said, 'Is that the best you've got? Trust me, that's nothing. You don't want to mess with me, Rion. You'll regret it. You don't know the trouble I can cause.' She turned on her heel and walked away.

My anger was quickly replaced by a sense of unease. What did she mean by that? She couldn't possibly know who I really was. I dismissed the thought. She couldn't do or say anything to hurt me. She was a bully, and I knew that underneath, all bullies were cowards.

But I had to admit that she was right about one thing. I might not have initiated that kiss, but I didn't stop it either.

# Chapter Seventeen

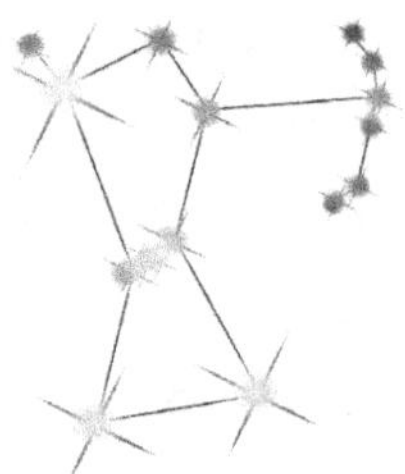

So you're Zoe's friend.' I felt Mrs Stewart's cool eyes appraise me. 'Her mother told me you're quite accomplished.'

'That's kind of her,' I said. Last year, I would've said she was correct. In fact, I would've said I wasn't just accomplished; I was *extremely* accomplished. But now I was more humble. I realised that knowledge was more than just facts.

Mrs Stewart gave a half smile and said, 'Let's just say you're probably smarter than Zoe, which wouldn't be hard. Emerson is the type of boy who needs to be challenged intellectually.'

Already I was beginning to dislike this woman. I was about to say something, but she didn't give me a chance.

'Here's the schedule for the evening. I understand you play chess adequately. Do you speak any foreign languages?'

'*Nin hau. Xinghui,*' I said in response. Did this woman really think she could intimidate me?

She raised her eyebrows. 'Japanese?'

'Mandarin Chinese, which you and Emerson obviously don't speak.'

'Well, there isn't much need of that here,' she said.

'Really? Despite the fact that China is one of our biggest trading partners, and Chinese tourists make up a significant percentage of visitors to this country?' I enjoyed her look of discomfort. 'Never mind, I understand that Emerson speaks French. *Bonjour, Madame. Comment allez-vous ce soir?*'

'*Bien,*' she said, in a flustered sort of way.

'Ah, *vous parlez français?*'

'*Un peu,*' she said. 'But it's not me you're here to practise with, it's Emerson. I'll just go and get him.' She made a hasty exit down the hallway.

I smiled and shook my head. She was no challenge at all.

I'd brushed up on my basic French in the hour or so after I accepted the babysitting job, and although I was by no means bilingual, I felt I could carry on a basic conversation. I was betting it was more than Mrs Stewart could do.

I looked around the pristine, utilitarian family room. This was a place Archimedes would approve of, but was it the right environment for a child? I was beginning to understand what Zoe was talking about.

A pale blond child came into the room. Assessing him, I could see that he needed more vitamin D, more exercise, and perhaps a couple of kilos more weight.

His face broke out into a smile when he saw me. 'I heard you're brilliant at chess.'

His mother frowned. 'Emerson, is that the way we greet people?'

His smile disappeared in an instant. 'No, Mummy.' She stood waiting. He held out a little hand and greeted me in French.

I shook it and answered him.

'Your accent is very good,' he said.

That was due to YouTube videos and having a good ear for languages, but I said nothing. I suspected Mrs Stewart was more than a little impressed with me and I didn't want anything to spoil that.

'I can see you two are going to get along well. Now, Emerson, don't forget your yoga exercises before bed. It may help you to sleep better. And if you wake up during the night, try reading your French storybook rather than coming into me. Mummy needs her sleep, too, doesn't she?'

His little face turned paler, if that was possible, and he nodded.

'Good. Well, I'll be off now.' She bent her cheek to Emerson, who gave it a quick peck.

She straightened up, and said to Rion, 'I won't be too late, around ten o'clock. I have an urgent meeting with a client, and when you're a senior lawyer in the firm, well, what can you do?' She shrugged and turned down the hall, her high heels echoing on the tiles. The front door closed behind her.

I turned to the boy beside me. I hadn't had much to do with children—actually, nothing—and I wondered how I was going to cope with a six year old, even a smart six year old. He was looking at me with his head to one side, assessing me in much the same way that his mother had. So far his attitude seemed positive, and I hoped that would continue.

'So, Emerson, what's first on our list?'

He gave a heavy sigh and sat down on the sofa, his short legs not touching the floor. 'French conversation, but I'm tired of speaking French. I had to learn French verbs all afternoon and I've had enough.'

I sat down beside him, prepared to compromise. 'Well, we had a conversation in French when we met, so maybe we can tick that off the list. We could do something else, like play a game of chess.'

'Are you really good at chess? Honestly?'

'Let's find out. Where's the set?'

I'd expected Emerson to have a basic knowledge of the game, but he surprised me by how well he could play. He was a strategic thinker and quick to catch on. I didn't let him win. But although I could have beaten him quickly, I kept the game going for an hour. At least that way he'd have some sense of accomplishment.

When I finally checkmated him, he looked at me and said, 'You could've won seven moves ago, why didn't you?'

I smiled. 'It was more fun. And this way we both get a chance to practise.'

'Zoe said you knew how to have fun.'

Zoe seemed to have said a lot about me.

'Do you?' Emerson's voice interrupted my thoughts.

'Pardon?'

'Do you know how to have fun?' He was looking at me with a serious expression on his face.

'I didn't always know how, but I learnt.'

'How?'

I thought for a moment and then felt my face break out in a smile. 'Zoe and I went bowling once and we had a lot of fun. We didn't even worry about who won. We didn't know how to bowl very well and we made a lot of mistakes, but we just laughed at them.'

I remembered that night with crystal clarity—not that I forgot anything ever, but that memory stood out: it was the first time I kissed Zoe.

'I've never been bowling,' he said. 'I'd like to go sometime, if Mummy lets me. She doesn't like me to go where there are a lot of people. She says I might pick up something and get sick.'

I was starting to feel really sorry for this kid. 'Do you play any sports at all, Emerson?'

'I do yoga and tai chi, and I've had some private swimming lessons in our pool. Dad says when I'm older he'll teach me how to play golf. Mummy says maybe I can take tennis lessons next year, if my health improves. I'm very delicate, you know.' He looked at me with his earnest eyes.

Perhaps, I thought, he wouldn't be quite so delicate if his mother let him play outside more and study less. I was surprised at myself. Last year I probably would have thought Mrs Stewart was a perfect mother and that no one could study too much. But I'd learnt a lot since then. And even though I didn't know a lot about children, Emerson didn't seem all that happy to me.

'Do you know how to play snap?' he asked.

I shook my head, thinking it must be some complicated intellectual game.

'I can teach you.' He opened a drawer in the coffee table and took out a pack of cards.

'Great, I'd love to learn,' I said.

Half an hour later, after a lot of excited shouting and slapping of hands over the cards, we stopped for a break.

'That was fun,' I said, and meant it.

'I'm really hungry.' Emerson flopped back on the couch.

Uh-oh. Zoe had told me this was how the trouble had started last time.

He must have read the expression on my face because he said, 'Don't worry, I'm not going to be naughty. There's no gelato left. And Dad must've finished the chocolate because there's none of that left either. I checked. But sometimes, if I'm really, really hungry, like famished, Mummy lets me have a healthy snack. And you know what? I think I'm hypoglycaemic right now because I feel faint. Although I haven't been tested for that yet. But I should eat something, just in case.'

He was one clever little human. 'Okay, let's check out the fridge. I wouldn't want you getting sick.' It didn't bother me one iota what Mrs Stewart would think.

We found some black grapes and rice crackers and brought them to the family room.

'I wish I could have something sweet, but I guess this'll have to do.' Emerson took a grape and popped it in his mouth.

'Hang on, ' I said, suddenly remembering the muesli bar I'd bought today but hadn't had time to eat. I reached into my pocket and brought it out. 'It's sweet, but healthy, too,' I said, giving it to him. 'No added sugar.'

His face lit up as he ripped off the wrapping and carefully broke it in two, giving me one of the halves.

'That's okay,' I said, 'you have it. I'm good with the grapes and crackers.'

'No, it's more fun when you share. That's what Giselle says.'

'Who's Giselle?'

'Our au pair. She's gone to France to see her family. I hope she comes back soon.' His face was wistful. 'She says I'm her special friend. I know special sometimes means different, but I don't mind when Giselle says it because I knew she likes me.'

'There's nothing wrong with being different, Emerson.'

'Yes, there is. I'm not the same as everyone else. Mummy says it, Dad sometimes says it, and everyone knows it. All the kids at school think I'm weird. No one wants to be my friend. Not that I care. They're all stupid, anyway. I'm a billion times smarter than they are, a *trillion* times.' He kicked the side of the sofa with his feet.

His words hit me hard. In many ways Emerson and I were similar.

'You wouldn't understand,' he said. 'Nobody does.'

'Yes, Emerson, actually I do understand,' I said. 'I'm different, too.'

He turned his face up to examine me. 'You don't look different. I mean, I know you're smart, but you also seem kind of … normal.'

And that, I thought, was one of the biggest compliments anyone had ever given me.

I tried to explain. 'Yes, I am smart, smarter than most people, but it took me a while to realise that's not everything. I had to learn how to be normal. Zoe helped me with that.'

'I think I like Zoe,' Emerson said.

I smiled. 'I do, too.'

'Is she your girlfriend?'

'No,' I said sadly.

'Why not? She likes you and you like her. What's the problem?'

How could I answer that? I tried. 'We're friends. But we're not much alike. I'm too different for her to like me.'

'See, I told you being different was no good,' he said, his voice quavering.

I realised my stupid mistake. And I'd said I was smart. I tried to fix things. 'I didn't mean it that way, Emerson. I just meant Zoe and I are from different places. We don't always understand each other's ways.'

'Where are you from?' he asked.

I hesitated. 'Far away.'

'Where? I do know my geography,' he said, staring at me with his wide intelligent eyes. 'What country are you from?'

I couldn't answer him.

He waited for a moment, and then said, 'Have you escaped from jail?'

I laughed. 'No.'

He narrowed his eyes. 'Are you an illegal immigrant?'

I could just imagine his mother asking something like that. I shook my head.

'So you're from another country, right?'

'Sort of,' I said.

'Sort of … hey, are you from another world?'

Now that was something no adult would ever ask. But kids, I guessed they had bigger imaginations. I struggled to find an answer that wouldn't be an outright lie. But Emerson, who must have had some sort of sixth sense, didn't give me time.

'You're an alien. I knew it. No one else could be so smart. That's why you beat me at chess.' He looked at me triumphantly.

I wanted to say no, but I couldn't. And what harm could it do? After all, he was only six and no one would believe him if he told anyone. So I nodded.

'What planet are you from?'

And that was just the beginning of the questions.

The 'schedule' was abandoned for the rest of the evening. Emerson had an insatiable curiosity and wanted to know everything about my world, especially our space mission where we inhabited hosts and learned about their ways. I tried to explain it simply, in words he'd understand, but I needn't have worried. He was a smart kid, and he took on faith a lot that adults would have been dubious about.

'I'd love to go to your planet, but I'd really love to be one of those bubble things you were and find out lots of things about different people. I wish I was like you, Rion, even though you're not a bubble any more.'

I'd finally gotten him to bed—way past his bedtime—and was trying to settle him before his mother came home. I sat down on his bed. 'You are like me, Emerson. We're both a bit different and that's okay, right?'

He nodded.

'But you can't tell anyone I'm an alien. That's just our secret.'

'Of course, I know that. They wouldn't understand, just like people don't always understand *me*. But am I really the only person who knows? Not even Zoe?'

I shook my head, and felt a lump in my throat. 'Not even her,' I said after a moment.

'So that makes us friends, doesn't it?'

'Absolutely,' I said.

'I won't ever tell your secret.'

I held up my hand. 'Friends. High-five.'

His little hand reached up and slapped mine, and his face broke out in a grin.

I stood up. 'And now you'd better go to sleep before your mother comes home. Otherwise she'll never look after you again.'

Emerson snuggled down in the bed. 'I'm good at pretending to sleep. You can turn off the light if you want. I don't mind. I'm just going to think about your planet up there in the stars.'

I turned off the light. 'Goodnight, Emerson.'

I was about to leave the room when his sleepy voice said, 'Next time you come, you can bring Zoe if you like. I don't mind.'

'Thanks, pal.' I said.

I was smiling to myself as I went down the stairs. I hadn't been lying to Emerson. In many ways he and I were very alike. Who would have thought that the person I had most in common with on Earth was a six-year-old boy?

# Chapter Eighteen

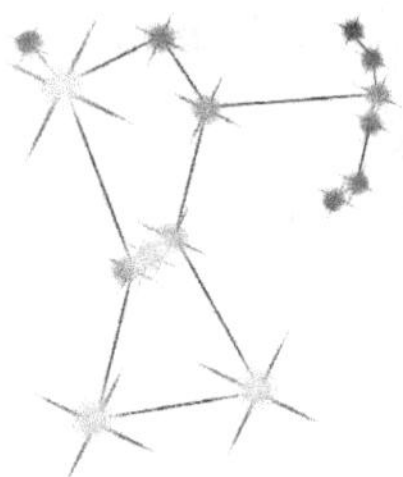

I looked in the mirror and sighed. Then I rolled up the waistband of my pencil skirt so it wasn't too long and let the navy-blue satiny shell I was wearing fall over it. I was going for sophisticated; instead I got office girl.

For the first time in a while I actually cared about my appearance, and I wasn't sure why. Harry was still just my friend, and Rion was … well, I wasn't sure what Rion was. Even Lou was going to look good today, especially since I'd given her a few tips on makeup and how to style her hair. Too bad I couldn't do the same for myself.

Hmmm. I'd given myself an idea. I ducked into Mum's room and grabbed her dangly gold earrings and bangles, then slipped on my black high heels. Better. At least my hair was shiny and straight, thanks to Mum's new straightener, and I'd finally mastered the art of applying mascara. I grabbed my clutch purse and headed downstairs.

Mum and Dad were in the lounge watching the news.

'You look really nice, dear,' Mum said. Then she looked at me more carefully. 'Hang on, don't I recognise those earrings?'

I gave her my sweetest smile. 'I was going to ask you. You don't mind, do you, Mum?'

She shook her head, smiling. 'But next time perhaps you could ask me before you borrow them.'

Dad looked at Mum and said, 'Who is this sophisticated young woman? Do we know her?'

'Ha-ha, Dad. Okay, Mum, we'd better get going. Oh, and I'll drive.'

'I think it would be better if Mum drove, don't you?' Dad said anxiously. 'It's not safe to drive in high heels, especially if you're still learning.'

'I'll take them off, and I'm an excellent driver, aren't I, Mum?'

'She'll be fine, dear. It's not far,' Mum said to Dad, grabbing the keys from her bag. He opened his mouth to protest, but Mum saved the day by quickly adding, 'Come on, Zoe, you don't want to be late.'

We headed out the door before Dad could think of anything else.

When we got to school, nearly everyone was there except Lou. Ms D was rushing around, checking who was here and if we had the first-aid kit (which apparently we couldn't go anywhere without, though I failed to see what kind of medical emergency would happen on a trip to the theatre, except perhaps a condition of chronic boredom) and was generally acting all teacher-y and In Charge. I thought someone ought to remind her we were year twelves and not year eights, and in less than a year we would be out of school and into the real world. But that was Ms D.

Then, just before we had to pile into the minibus, Lou's mum drove up and Lou got out. She looked amazing. With just a little makeup, and her hair swept back to reveal cheekbones that no one even knew she had, she looked so different from the mousy little everyday Lou. And I'd been right about the dress; it did bring out the blue of her eyes.

Maybe I should consider a career as a stylist, I thought. I sure have managed to transform Lou.

And I wasn't the only one who noticed. I wouldn't say Harry's jaw dropped, but he was definitely staring, and so was Rion. I noticed a few other guys looking her way as well.

I went over to her. 'You look great, Lou.'

She turned her shiny eyes on me and said, 'It's all because of you, Zoe. Thank you so much.' She gave me a hug.

I shrugged. 'No worries.'

We went over to our group.

'Wow, Lou,' Harry said. 'You look nice.'

'Yes, you look really pretty,' Rion said.

Lou blushed. It was probably the first time any boys had paid her a compliment.

'I hate dressing up,' Kerri said. She was wearing a yellow blouse buttoned all the way to the top, a plaid skirt and sensible flats. But at least she was carrying a handbag instead of a book. 'It's such a waste of time and effort.'

'Not really,' Rion said. 'You're going to see a world-famous play by one of the greatest playwrights that ever lived. Surely that's worth dressing up for.'

He was looking pretty spiffy himself in a black shirt, red tie and dark trousers. And Harry was looking hot, too, in a light green shirt that made his hazel eyes look even greener.

'I just hope I understand what's going on,' Lou said. 'Even though I've read the play, it's the language that gets me. I don't understand it half the time.'

'I can sit next to you and explain it to you, if you like,' Rion said.

'Oh, that'd be great,' Lou said, looking up at him.

'Just don't talk all the way through it. I hate when people do that,' Kerri said. 'It's so distracting and irritating.'

'I'll try not to, but sit somewhere else if it bothers you,' Rion said. He turned to smile at me. 'You should probably sit next to us too, Zoe. You'd probably be able to explain it better than me anyway. You're so good at English.'

'You'll manage,' Harry said to him.

'Would everybody please line up to get on board,' Ms D called, clipboard in hand. 'I'll check off your names as you get in.'

Harry moved next to me as we shuffled into line. 'Hey, you look pretty nice tonight, Zoe.'

An afterthought, but I'd take it. At least someone had noticed.

We found our seats, and within a few moments the bus moved forward with a jerk. We were off.

When we were finally settled in the theatre, somehow I'd ended up next to Harry, with Kerri, Lou and Rion on the other side of him. I didn't mind. It was nice for Lou to feel special for a change, and it was always easy for me to talk to Harry.

Jas had arrived only just in time to get in before the curtain lifted. She made an entrance in a hot-pink sleeveless dress and red killer heels. If I hadn't known her, and you'd told me she was twenty-five, I would've believed you. And, amazingly, she had Chad in tow. She must have persuaded him to give up football training for the night. They had seats in front of us and I noticed she totally ignored Rion as she passed him, although Chad gave him a scowl. What's up there, I wondered.

The play wasn't quite as boring as I'd expected, and it was kind of exciting to be in a real theatre and see actual people saying the lines we had struggled to understand. The costumes, sets and actions all helped make it more understandable.

During the witches' scene, I whispered, 'I can just see Jas casting a spell or two with them.'

'Nah,' he whispered back, 'she's more the Lady Macbeth type, except she'd probably—'

'Take the crown from Duncan for herself,' I said.

We shared a smile. That was the thing I liked about Harry. We knew each other so well that we could finish each other's sentences.

Rion was busy whispering to Lou, no doubt about the play. At least she looked happy.

After the performance, when we were outside the theatre waiting for the minibus, Jas and Chad came out like royalty. People actually moved aside for them. Then Chad caught sight of Rion and headed purposefully towards him.

Jas, who was trailing behind him, said in a very unconvincing voice, 'Leave it, babe. He's not worth it.' He ignored her, as I was sure she wanted him to.

Stopping in front of Rion, Chad put his hands on his hips. 'Hey, Rion,' he said, 'stay away from my girlfriend.'

Rion gave Chad a cool, appraising look. 'You've got it all wrong. I'm not the slightest bit interested in your girlfriend.'

'Oh yeah?' Chad took a step closer, but Rion didn't back away. 'Is that why you kissed her last week?'

'I think you need to talk to your girlfriend. She was the one who kissed me,' Rion said.

'You son of a —' *Thump*. Chad punched Rion in the jaw and he staggered backwards. Harry moved to his side quickly and I was close behind him.

'Chad, cool it, man,' Harry said, as he stepped between them. 'Rion, are you okay?' he said.

Rion was holding his chin and his eyes were stormy. He moved forward, but I put a hand on his arm. 'Don't,' I whispered. He stopped, but his whole body was tensed, ready to move forward at any time.

Everyone else just looked on in shock.

Ms D finally noticed something was going on and rushed over. 'Stop this right now. You two, over here, the rest of you on the bus, *now.*'

Rion shook off my hand. 'Go on, I'm okay.'

I moved away reluctantly, looking over my shoulder to make sure Rion was calming down. I'd never seen him so angry. But then a hazy memory came back to me … there was a party and I'd left Rion there. When he'd caught up with me he was pretty agro at being left behind, but I couldn't remember why. The details escaped me.

I got on the bus and sat down, then I looked out the window. Ms D had pulled Chad and Rion aside and was talking to them. She had that angry-teacher stance, and who could blame her. This didn't look good for any future excursions she might want to plan.

Jas was looking teary, or trying to. Then Ms D sent Rion to the bus, and indicated that Jas and Chad should leave. As both Rion and Ms D climbed aboard, I looked at Jas. She smiled back at me, and I was certain then that she had planned the whole thing.

Rion sat next to Kerri, who had somehow managed to fit a book inside her handbag and was reading. I thought she must be the only one on the bus who didn't have the slightest interest in what had happened. And maybe that's why Rion sat next to her, because it was clear he didn't want to talk.

I wasn't so keen on talking, either. Now that I was over the shock of what had happened and I could see that Rion was all right physically, something else was in my thoughts. Rion and Jas had kissed—again. And for some reason that was the thing that upset me the most.

When I arrived home, I was in no mood to see Archimedes sitting on the leather lounge, flicking through the channels on the TV and looking bored.

'Oh, there you are at last. I have been waiting precisely eleven minutes and fourteen, fifteen sec—' He stopped and looked at me. 'What happened? Have you had an accident?'

'Yeah, an accident,' I said. 'Don't want to talk about it.'

'Interesting. You use an emergency code red to contact me about a pimple, but now there's blood on your mouth and bruising on your cheek and you don't want to talk about it. I really don't think this human life suits you.'

I sat down on the chair opposite him. 'What do you want, Archimedes?' I said, not too politely.

'What I want is to leave this tiresome job as your guardian, and this burdensome body, to return forever to my former perfect state of consciousness and intellectual pursuit. Luckily, my sacrifices will not be needed for much longer.'

'Are you saying you won't be my guardian anymore?' That seemed too much to hope for.

He looked at me. 'It has been decided. You have compromised the integrity of this experiment. I knew you would do so eventually, but I wasn't expecting it so soon. However, by the look of you I'd say I've come just in time to save you.'

'What do you mean?' Alarm bells started ringing inside me.

'I did warn you,' he said.

He was testing my patience to the limit. 'Would you please just tell me what's going on?'

'You told that child who you are. If he tells anyone, your secret is out. It's too great a risk. You can't possibly stay here any longer. So, you will be delighted and relieved to know that you're coming back. This whim to be a human has ended.'

'Pardon?' I wasn't quite sure I was hearing him correctly.

'We've worked out a way for you to dematerialise and become pure consciousness again. You will be free of your tiresome organic existence and its limitations.' He smiled benignly at me.

'But I was meant to be here for life, until I died. And how do you know what I told Emerson anyway?'

'You should be pleased. Your existence now will not be terminated after a mere sixty or seventy years. After you've had suitable time to recover from this arduous ordeal, you will find another host. And as to knowing what you said, I am your guardian, whether I'm in this body or not. I know everything. Otherwise how would I look out for you?' He frowned. 'I had thought you would be more grateful than this.'

I could hardly find the words to answer him. Finally, I said the one thing that I hoped would save me. 'But I've been human for too long. You said that three hours was the limit. I've been in this organic state for over eight months.'

Archimedes gave an elaborate sigh. 'I told you,' he said, 'we've worked out a way around that. Before you became human, we never worried about the problems involved with being in an organic state for extended periods of time. It wasn't a priority because it was not considered that anyone would want that. But when you told that child you were an alien, I realised something had to be done, and urgently. I let our people know, and we've worked out a way to increase the time period to twelve months. This means that you can dematerialise now, since you've been an organic for less than a year. Lucky you. Your time as a human is at an end. You've been given a second chance.'

I felt as if I was in a disaster movie, with everything crashing down around me. 'But I don't want it to come to an end.'

I realised that was the truth, despite everything that happened. I wanted a chance for Zoe to realise she liked me, even if she didn't remember our connection. I wanted to finish the school year with her, go to university, for Zoe and I to explore the world together. I could see Paris firsthand with Zoe, we could go on a gondola in Venice, we could … A hundred things flashed through my brain.

Most importantly, I wanted to feel her soft lips again, to hold her close, to hear her heart beat in time with mine. I wasn't ready to give all that up yet.

'It's too late,' Archimedes said. 'The decision has been made for you. You will finish up at school next week and we will make up some pretext that you and I are going on another adventure. Let's say Alaska, that's far enough away. I hear the northern lights are fabulous. Any photographer worth his salt would surely want to photograph them.'

I looked at him, trying to process everything he was saying. 'Who exactly made this decision? I was given a choice. You can't just take that away from me.' Archimedes looked uncomfortable. My suspicions heightened. 'You did, didn't you?'

He gave a shrug. 'I may have suggested it. I've been worried for quite some time. When we went to dinner with the Brennans I couldn't help but notice the closeness between you and that girl. Even though I'd erased her memories, I could tell that the connection between you had not been totally severed. She might remember who you are. She would tell her friends, who would tell their friends, and so on. And even if that didn't happen, I believe it's only a matter of time before you tell Zoe yourself. After all, you told a six-year-old boy who isn't even your host. Thanks to you, our secret identity, which we have guarded over the centuries, has now been revealed. The only reason our hosts have kept quiet for so long is because they haven't wanted to appear crazy. And also because of the benefits we've given them, of course.'

I got up and paced the room, more furious than I'd ever been with this 'guardian' of mine. When I felt able to speak, I whirled around to face him. 'The only reason you want me to cease being human is because of the inconvenience to yourself. The rest is just a whole lot of hot air. You never wanted to be my guardian in the first place.'

Archimedes frowned. 'It's only too obvious to me how much this human existence has degraded you. You need what these humans call an 'intervention', and the sooner the better, in my opinion.'

I made a supreme effort to control the temper that was raging through me. I took a couple of deep breaths before saying, 'I don't want to stop being human. In fact,

I refuse to. You are not highly enough ranked to force me, Archimedes. This decision, which you have made and then passed along to our supervisor, is flawed and made out of self-interest. Let's deal with the real issue here. If you don't want to be my guardian, fine. Disappear. It's not like anyone will notice you're gone, anyway. By the end of this year I'll be eighteen and legally independent. But I won't be forced to leave this life just because it's inconvenient for you. Is that clear?'

Archimedes stood up and came to face me, his arms folded across his chest. He was shorter than me, but I felt his anger, too. It was cool, but no less intense for that.

'What's clear to me is that you have taken leave of your senses. You're making all sorts of false accusations against me when I have only your best interests in mind. Can you deny that you revealed your identity to a human? Someone who was not even a host to you, as Zoe was?'

'Even if I did, it wouldn't make any difference. Emerson won't tell anyone, and even if he does no one will believe him. And Zoe would never tell anyone. She was always the one to caution me against revealing my identity. After all, it was *you* who gave me the choice about whether to take away her memories. You were willing to take that risk then, why not now?'

'I didn't fully realise the dangers. I do now. She cares too much and so do you. Nothing good ever comes from such intense feelings.'

'She cares nothing about me anymore and she remembers nothing about her feelings for me. And that's harder to bear than I realised. I was even going to ask you to restore her memories.'

Archimedes gave me an incredulous look. 'Even if I could, I wouldn't. Not now. But thankfully I can't. What's done is done. The only way Zoe will remember anything is if those memories come back naturally.'

The weight of those words hit me hard.

'And,' Archimedes continued, 'what kind of position have you put Emerson in? Knowing something like that and not being able to tell anyone.'

'I was trying to help him, to let him know he wasn't the only one who felt different from everyone around him.'

'So you told him you're an alien, and that knowledge will make him even *more* different. If he tells anyone they'll think he's mentally unbalanced. How is that going to help him?'

Archimedes' words hit home. But he wasn't finished.

'And as for Zoe, if you become close and then have a falling out, are you sure she won't use her knowledge against you? It is the way of humans, you know. They can be petty and shortsighted. They hardly ever act for the greater good.'

That was one thing I could answer. 'Zoe is a good person. You've met her family, Archimedes. They're all good people.'

'I admit Zoe's mother is a singular female.' Archimedes eyes softened. 'Her husband is somewhat dull, but I could detect no real malice.' He turned from me and walked over to the window, looking up at the night sky. 'But they are human and therefore fallible.'

'And we aren't, Archimedes? Despite our intelligence, we've made mistakes. As you've just pointed out, I certainly have. Our people are by no means perfect. It took thousands of years, almost as many wars, and the near destruction of our planet before we were able to have a more enlightened approach to civilisation. And even now, can you say we're infallible?'

He turned to face me again. 'All the more reason to return to us,' he said. 'You were not destined for this life. Surely you realise that by now.' His eyes, for once, were kind. I realised he really believed this was the best thing for me. 'Being human, mixing with them, it's not good for us, and not good for them, either.'

I shook my head. 'It's too late, Archimedes. I'm more human than alien now. Life is messy here, but it's real.

I've never felt more, or experienced more than I have in the last eight months. When we're with our hosts we only experience life secondhand. We exist, but we don't truly live. I would rather live one human life here than an eternity as what I was. That's my choice, and you have no right to take it from me.'

Archimedes looked at me sadly. 'The decision has already been made. You will return to us at the end of next week. Say your goodbyes and make your peace. It is over.'

I refused to accept it. 'I want to talk to our supervisor. Tell him.'

'I can tell you right now,' he said, 'it will be useless. Once he has made up his mind, he rarely changes it.'

'I have to try. Promise me you'll pass on my request. You owe me that, Archimedes.'

'I've fulfilled my obligation to you, Orion. I owe you nothing.'

'That's not true. You admitted you were behind all this. You've never believed in this experiment and you were just waiting for me to slip up so you could find a way to end it. You haven't been perfect yourself, Archimedes. You owe me a second chance. Ask our supervisor to meet with me. Let me at least talk to him.'

He said nothing for a moment, looking more tired than I had ever seen him. Then he said, 'Yes, yes, all right,

I will ask. Not that it will do much good. I need to go back now. Someone will be in touch. I have tried my best, Orion, whether you believe it or not.'

All I said was, 'Don't forget that you've promised, Archimedes.' In our culture, a promise was sacred. We were bound by every moral value we held to honour it.

He nodded to me, too tired to speak any more. Before my eyes, he slowly dissolved and disappeared.

# Chapter Nineteen

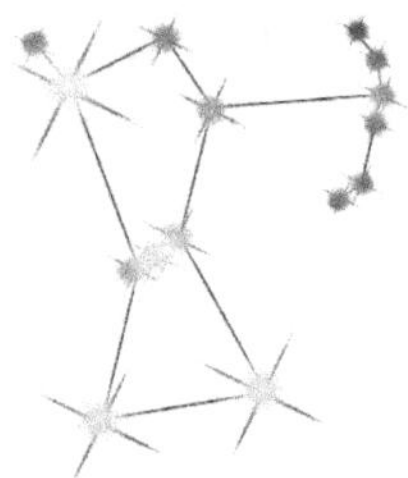

Thoughts were whirling around in my head like clothes in a spin dryer. I still couldn't get over the fact that Chad Everett had punched Rion. But … Rion and Jas had kissed. Whoever started it was kind of irrelevant.

But why should I care? It's nothing to me. I needed to sleep. I scrunched up the pillow, then turned over and scrunched it again.

Jas was a piece of work, no doubt about it. I saw the way she looked after Chad punched Rion. She was deliberately stirring, I knew it, but why? Did she really like Rion, or did she just enjoy boys fighting over her?

Once Jas and I had been friends, and there were times when she wasn't totally horrible. She stood up for me once against Chelsea, who'd called me a loser. 'Leave her alone,' Jas had said. 'At least she's got a brain.'

Okay, kind of mean to Chelsea, who was dumb as. But still, very occasionally Jas was okay. So, I didn't really think she wanted World War III to break out over her, even though she was clearly enjoying it.

My only other conclusion was that she really did like Rion. After all, he was hot, brainy, and I was discovering he wasn't so bad when you got to know him. But did he like Jas? Maybe. I had to admit they suited each other in a looks-and-brains kind of way. More than I did. So why should I care, I asked myself again. Good luck to them.

This time I was definitely going to sleep.

Except that I didn't, at least not for ages.

And when I woke up the next morning I felt like I had about a million hangovers and was at least fifty years old. Not that I'd ever had a hangover or anything. Well, except maybe that once when I was twelve and Mandy, my best friend, raided her parents' alcohol cupboard and gave me a cocktail with about six different ingredients. I thought I was going to die.

So yes, except for the sick part, I felt kind of like that.

I glared at the sunshine streaming in through the window. When I had the energy to move, I was going to close those curtains and pull down the blind. I hated mornings. I was so glad we had a holiday today. Putting the pillow over my head, I closed my eyes. That lovely, heavy sleepy sensation was engulfing me when my phone rang, jerking me awake again. I grabbed it, thinking it might be Lou, or maybe Harry suggesting a day at the beach. Maybe his mum had lent him the car.

But when I looked at the caller ID, I saw Rion's name. I hesitated. Part of me wanted to see if he was okay or not, but the rest of me still wondered why he had kissed Jas. Maybe he should call *her* if he wanted someone to talk to. I wasn't jealous, no way. Or was I?

Before I could make up my mind the phone stopped ringing, and a few seconds later I heard the ping of a text. Sighing, I sat up and looked at my phone again. What was so majorly important at this time of day? All the texts were from Rion.

*Zoe, I need to talk to you.*

*Please answer.*

*Something has happened.*

That last one stopped me. This sounded serious. I called him.

'Hey.'

'Zoe.' His voice sounded relieved. 'Thanks for calling.'

'What's up? Are you in trouble?' I wondered if there'd been some fallout from the school over what had happened with Chad.

'I'm leaving.'

'What?' I felt like someone had punched me in the stomach. I wasn't sure how I felt about Rion, but even so I didn't want him to leave.

'Archimedes has to leave and I'm going with him.'

'But you said he wasn't even your uncle.'

'No, but he's my guardian so I have to go with him. And this time I won't be able to come back.'

'So you don't want to go?'

'No, of course not, I'm going to try to stay, but … I don't know if I'll succeed.'

'Why does he want to do that? I mean, it's your senior year and everything.'

'He thinks it's best for me. It's complicated.'

'Yeah, it usually is with you.' I was losing my patience with that line. 'I don't see how I can help you, especially since I don't really know much about the situation.'

'Can we meet? I want to talk to you face to face. I want to tell you … everything. I might not get another chance.'

Rion sounded desperate, and I knew I had to hear him out. I wanted to understand him, and maybe then I could understand myself. 'Okay, but this time I want the truth. All of it.'

'Thank you.'

'How about we meet in our boatshed? It's quiet and it might be easier to talk there.' Why I picked that place, I wasn't sure. But it seemed right, somehow.

'Perfect. I'll be there in about fifteen minutes.'

'Yeah. The key's over the door.'

'I know. I remember.'

I lay back on my bed, wondering about that last remark. When had he been there before? What was the truth about Rion? Even though I was curious, there was also a small part of me that was afraid. What if I didn't like what he had to say? And what if he really was in serious trouble?

I showered, got dressed and slipped out of the house. Running across the grass, I went into the shed where our cabin cruiser was stored. Rion was already waiting for me on the deck of the boat.

'You came.' I could hear the relief in his voice.

'I said I would, didn't I?' I climbed up onto the boat and stood next to him. 'Let's sit in the cabin.'

We sat down on opposite seats, and I could see the strain on his face.

I said, 'So?'

He didn't answer for a moment or two, and then he said, 'I'm sorry I lied to you and your parents about Archimedes being my uncle and going to the Amazon rainforest.'

'Why did you? What are you trying to hide?'

'I was trying to protect you.'

'From what, an alien invasion or something?'

He gave a hollow laugh. 'You don't know how close you are to the truth.'

I was starting to lose my patience. 'I'm not in the mood for jokes.'

'Just how much do you remember about me from last year, Zoe?'

I concentrated, trying to remember, and a few hazy details came back to me. 'Your mum went north with her boyfriend and left you behind. You needed a place to stay for a while and my parents took you in. Then Archimedes came and took you away. So if he isn't your uncle, who is he?'

'I'll tell you in a minute, but what I meant was, what do you remember about us? You and me?'

I looked at him, puzzled by the question and not sure of its relevance. 'We didn't get along at times, you know that, but everyone keeps telling me how close we were and I don't remember that at all. Were we?'

He leaned forward and said, 'Zoe, look at me, really look at me, and think hard. Do you remember any connection between us at all?'

His dark eyes rested on mine, searching. Some flicker, some wisp of a memory seemed to float in the back of my mind, just out of reach. Being here in the boat beside him seemed familiar. 'Did you go out with my family on the boat or something?'

He shook his head. 'We've been on this boat before, yes, but only here in the shed. The first time was when I came home with you, before your parents agreed that I could stay with you. I slept here until we could come up with a story to tell your family.'

'What do you mean? Why would we need any story?'

'Because if we'd told them the truth they would think I was insane. You told me at the time that they might send me away or something. Sometimes I wonder if I should've let them.'

I was starting to get worried. What sort of trouble was Rion in? 'What happened?' I said. 'You're not into drugs, are you?'

'No, no nothing like that, I don't even drink.' Rion sat back and crossed his arms, obviously struggling with something. Then he said, 'I'm not the same as you or anyone here. I'm from another place. To be precise, another planet. It's in the constellation of Orion. That's why I called myself Rion. It reminded me of where I was from.'

Whoa, this was crazyland. I stood up, knocking my head on the low ceiling of the boat and feeling it rock. Like my world was being rocked at the moment. I took a deep breath and sat down again. 'Are you telling me you're an … alien?'

He nodded. 'Yes.'

'You're nuts.'

'No, just an alien.'

I looked at him, speechless.

'I know it's a shock to you, but I was hoping you would remember, at least a little.'

'Remember what? Seriously, Rion, this sounds bizarre. You can't really expect me to believe this.'

He was obviously unstable. Perhaps he had post-traumatic syndrome or something because of his mother leaving him. I tried to remain calm.

'Just hear me out. I'll tell you everything.'

He took my hands. I should have taken them away, but somehow I couldn't. He was a friend, however crazy, and I needed to be supportive. Besides, feeling his warm, strong hands in mine felt right.

He said, 'Do you remember the day we first met?'

I searched in my mind but the memory was hazy. 'Didn't we meet at the beach or something? It was cold and I really didn't want to be there, but my parents had gone on holiday and insisted on taking me with them.'

'Yes, it was at the beach, but it wasn't an ordinary encounter because I was … different.'

'No offence, Rion, but you've always been different.' It had always amazed me that someone who could look so hot could be such a geek.

'Yeah, I know, but I mean *really* different. I didn't have a physical body. I was an airborne conscious entity and I fell on you; then you became my host. We shared our thoughts. That was how we communicated. The intention was that I would be with you for the rest of your life. It's the way of our … people. Humans become our hosts. It's how we learn about your planet and expand our knowledge of the universe.'

I just looked at him. I wasn't sure if I was hearing correctly. 'That sounds very creepy.'

He gave a faint smile. 'You weren't exactly overjoyed, that's for sure. We didn't get on well at first. Not that I could blame you. Now that I know more about being human, I can understand why.'

'Okay, seriously? If this is true, and I'm not entirely convinced that you aren't crazy, then how come you're human now?' And looking so much better than a soap bubble, I thought irrelevantly.

'It was the night of the party when you were trying to convince Chad to like you. I came up with the crazy idea of materialising in a physical form so you could make him jealous. But when I tried to dematerialise again, I couldn't. I was stuck in my human form, and that's why we had to come up with a story to tell your parents so I'd have somewhere to stay.'

'So why don't I remember any of this?' That to me was the clincher. Not only was his story unbelievable, but I didn't remember a single thing about it.

He looked uncomfortable. 'Because when I left last year I told you I was going back to my people, but I didn't. I stayed human. And then Archimedes, who is also one of us, turned up as my uncle, and he told me I needed to go back to school to prepare myself for the human world. He also suggested he wipe your memories of my true identity to make things easier for everyone. I agreed, because I wanted you to be free.'

'Free of what?'

'Me. I cared about you and I think you cared about me, a little. I didn't think it was fair on you, because, well, because I'm an alien.'

I leaned my head back against the seat and closed my eyes. This was the most ridiculous story I'd ever heard. And yet, another part of me, buried deep inside my brain, told me that what Rion was saying wasn't totally a lie. There were some elements of truth, maybe. As for having had feelings towards him, that had me totally confused. I didn't dislike him anymore, and at times, especially lately, I felt that I could actually like him, and maybe as more than just a friend. But an alien?

'Zoe,' he said quietly after a while.

I sighed and opened my eyes. 'I'm sorry, Rion, I really am. I wish I could remember, but I can't. You have to admit it's one heck of a story.'

'I know. I was hoping that if I told you the whole story, your memories would come back.'

'Why are you telling me now?'

'Because I am going away, that part's true. Archimedes thinks I've been human long enough and to stay any longer wouldn't be wise. I don't want to go, but the choice has been taken away from me. I wanted you to know who I really am before I go. I hoped you'd remember that we were close once.'

He leaned forward, dropped my hands and put his own on my shoulders. 'I kissed you in this very place on your sixteenth birthday. Do you remember that?' His dark brown eyes, so close, looked into mine. I suddenly realised I wouldn't mind if he kissed me right now, alien or not.

I reached up and touched his cheek with my finger. I felt him shiver. 'I … I think I must have cared for you once, Rion. And maybe, in time, I'll remember everything that happened between us. I want to. But right now I know that I'm your friend. And friends tell each other the truth. I want to help you, and I'll be here for you.'

I paused, thinking about my next words. 'But please think about what you're saying. Maybe you really do believe that you're an alien. Maybe something happened when you were living with your mum that made you block out everything about your real life. Maybe that's why you invented this story. You should talk to my mum. She's a teacher and she knows professionals who understand that kind of stuff. She really likes you and she'd be happy to help you. Do you want me to ask her?'

I hated seeing the disappointment on his face. I wanted to throw my arms around him and tell him I didn't care if he thought he was an alien or not. I had felt our closeness and I wanted to feel it again. But that would be selfish. Rion needed help, and I couldn't turn away from that.

He looked away from me, brushing his eyes with his sleeve. 'No,' he said. 'And I'd appreciate it if you could keep all this to yourself. I don't want anyone else to know.'

'Rion, please, I'm on your side. I'm not judging. I want to help.'

He shook his head. 'Thanks, Zoe, but that's not what I need at all. I'm sorry to have burdened you with all this. I shouldn't have. I just hoped you'd remember. But now that I have told you, I'd appreciate if you didn't tell anyone else.'

'No, of course I won't, if that's what you want. But what do you want me to do? Please help me to understand.'

He shook his head. 'It doesn't matter now. I'll be gone soon anyway.'

'No. Don't go. Not now.'

'I might not have the choice, Zoe.'

Alarm bells rang inside me. 'Are you sure you can trust Archimedes? You don't have to go with him if you don't want to, especially if he's … unkind to you.'

'It's okay, Zoe. Archimedes might seem strange, but he is trustworthy. He has my best interests in mind, even though I don't agree with him. You don't have to worry about me.'

Then he gave me his crooked smile and I felt my heart go out to him. 'I should let you go,' he said. 'We probably won't have a chance to talk like this before I leave, so I'll say goodbye now. It's been the greatest experience of my existence knowing you, Zoe Brennan. I hope you have a wonderful life.' He reached over and moved a curl and then kissed my forehead lightly.

I felt the tears gather in my eyes and I closed them. 'No,' I whispered, 'don't say goodbye, not yet.' I felt him move away and opened my eyes. 'I want to remember so badly, Rion.'

He shook his head sadly. 'You probably never will. Archimedes did too good a job of removing your memories. I don't want to burden you, Zoe. It was bad enough when you knew I was an alien. That was always going to be a barrier between us. But now you think I'm crazy, and that's much worse. I won't do that to you.'

I started to speak, to protest, but before I could get the words out, he had stood and climbed up the cabin steps. With a light jump, he was off the boat.

I ran up the steps after him. 'No, please, wait,' I called, 'don't go.'

He didn't hear me. The shed door had closed behind him.

I got off the boat and rushed over to the door, wrenching it open. I ran outside and looked up and down the street. I couldn't see him anywhere. The sobs I'd been struggling to hold back burst out, but I wasn't sure who I was crying for, Rion or myself.

# Chapter Twenty

That night I looked out the window and saw the constellation of Orion. It had felt familiar to me before I heard what Rion had to say. Could there be some truth to what he had told me?

He had spoken of the connection between us, and there was something deep within me that told me that much at least was true. There, in the boat, I had realised something else. I really did care about Rion, and not just as a friend. And I didn't want him to go. Just the thought of not seeing him again made me heartsick.

But as for him being an alien … how could that possibly be true? I knew that *he* believed it. Now I had to decide if I could trust enough in his belief to overcome my own disbelief.

And now he was going away, again. But he didn't want to and that worried me. He was in his senior year and probably headed for a brilliant career because he was one of the smartest people I knew. But thanks to Archimedes he might not have a chance to finish his schooling—at least not this year.

He said he was going back to his people, whoever they were. That didn't sound good. The more I thought about it, the more worried I became. It wasn't right that he should have to go somewhere he didn't want to. But what could I do?

I thought maybe I should just forget about Rion and everything he'd told me. After all, he was going away and in all likelihood I wouldn't see him again.

I considered it for, like, a microsecond. Then a big *no way* bounced into my mind. Just thinking about never seeing Rion again made me feel hollow inside. And imagining something bad happening to him … well, I couldn't even go there.

I really wished I hadn't promised to tell anyone because I knew Mum would know what to do. I could just imagine her turning up on Rion's doorstep and demanding to speak to Archimedes. She wouldn't let him off. She would demand answers. When my mum thought a kid was at risk, she was like a tiger.

Then a thought, a crazy thought, entered my mind. Why couldn't I do that instead? I could talk to Archimedes myself and ask him just what he was thinking of, taking Rion away again in his senior year. I knew in Archimedes' eyes I was probably just a kid, but it might make him think twice, especially if he thought I would tell my parents.

I sat on my bed and drew my legs up to my chin, wrapping my arms around them. Maybe, just maybe, it could work. I'd have to go when Rion wasn't around because he'd probably tell me not to interfere. The only time I knew for sure that he wouldn't be home was during school. I had a spare last period on Monday. I could slip away without being noticed and scoot along to Rion's place before he got home. I had no idea if Archimedes would even be there, but it was worth a try.

My mind snapped to a decision. I'd go after school on Monday. I would rescue Rion from whatever kooky idea Archimedes had come up with. And maybe then Rion and I could work out what we meant to each other.

On Monday, I had second thoughts. Maybe confronting Archimedes wasn't such a great idea. What if he slammed the door in my face? What if he decided to ring my parents and tell them? That would go down well with them. Not. And anyway, I'd promised Rion I wouldn't tell them. How would he feel if they found out?

What if he just laughed at me and told me to get lost? What if he wasn't even home?

And here was the big one. When Rion found out, would he be angry with me for interfering?

I tried to stay out of his way on Monday, which wasn't hard because it seemed he was avoiding me, too. He didn't come and sit with our group at lunchtime, and other than give me a nod on the way to class he never said a word to me. It looked like he really didn't want to have anything to do with me anymore. That thought made me even more miserable. If I hadn't been planning to confront Archimedes, I would've talked to Rion, told him how I felt. But that would have to wait until I sorted things out.

And then I heard that he and Chad had been called up to the deputy principal's office to explain what had happened on Thursday night.

'I think Rion got off with a warning although, really, he didn't do anything,' Lou said at lunchtime. 'And Chad has a detention. Some people think he should've been suspended, but they let him off because his team has an early season game this week. I told Rion I thought it was totally unfair.'

'Well, he seems to have recovered now. He was fine in class when I talked to him,' Harry said.

What, was Rion talking to everyone now except me?

I looked over at Jas. She was the one who should've got the detention. Chad and Jas, and all her minions were laughing and talking as if nothing had happened. It wasn't right. She had deliberately stirred Chad up so he'd do something.

The day dragged on, and the closer it got to last period, the crazier the butterflies in my stomach became. Finally, I slipped out the school gate and headed for home at a near jog. I didn't have much time before school was over and Rion was home. I grabbed my helmet and wheeled my bike from the garage. It was quicker than walking.

The day was hot, and by the time I got there I was dripping with sweat. That's a good look for prissy Archimedes, I thought. He'd probably think I was just a stupid, emotional kid. Was I really doing the right thing?

Removing my helmet, I looped the strap over the handle bar and leaned my bike against the fence. Then, taking a deep breath, I went up to the door and knocked. The sound echoed inside. I waited. And waited. And waited.

Archimedes wasn't home. I felt like a balloon that had had the air taken out of it.

Glancing at my watch, I realised I didn't have much time to wait around. Maybe Archimedes was taking a nap or something. I moved to the bushes under the window and peered through the half-open vertical blinds.

The lounge room looked half empty, with just a white sofa and chair. It looked like they'd already started to pack up. What could have happened to make them decide to leave so suddenly? I started moving to another window to see if there was anything else, any clue as to what was going on.

I nearly jumped out of my skin when I heard the voice behind me. 'Can I help you?'

Turning around, I saw Archimedes by the front door, frowning at me. In his neat shirt and trousers, he looked like a businessman or maths teacher, anything but the sinister character I'd built up in my mind. And strangely, he had on the same clothes that he wore to dinner weeks ago. Didn't he own much clothing? Irrelevant, I told myself. Stick with the plan, Zoe.

'Hi,' I said, feeling that this wasn't the best way to meet him. I trudged awkwardly out of the bushes and stood on the path in front of him.

'Zoe?' he said in an abrupt way. 'What are you doing here?'

I took a deep breath and looked him straight in the eye. 'I came to see you. I want to talk to you. Can I come in?'

He looked surprised and I decided to take the initiative. The door was open behind him, so before he could change his mind I brushed passed him and went inside. 'Thanks,' I said. I couldn't believe I had just done that.

I went into the small lounge, hearing his footsteps behind me. It wasn't until I reached the chair that I turned around.

His eyebrows formed a line and I could see he was anything but pleased. 'You need to leave. Rion will be home from school soon and we have things to do.'

I sat down and looked up at him. 'I won't take long, but this is important.'

'I cannot imagine that you have anything to say to me that's important.'

Yup, he was just as charming as I remembered.

But he did sit down on the sofa. Now I just had to keep going before I lost my nerve.

'Rion told me you're taking him away again and that he doesn't want to go. He shouldn't be leaving in his senior year. Why are you doing this and where are you taking him?'

Archimedes looked shocked. Then he spoke. 'Rion is none of your concern. I'm his uncle and I have the right to make these decisions for him.'

'You're not his uncle. Who are you?' That was a strike home, I could tell.

'What has Orion been telling you? I hope you haven't believed his lies, because I can tell you right now, you can disregard them. I'm his legal guardian and that is that. And now, I think you'd better leave.'

I stayed firmly in my chair. 'You don't seem to have a very good opinion of him if you think he tells lies. Either that or maybe some of the things he told me are true. And anyway, next year he'll be eighteen and can make his own decisions. He doesn't want to go wherever you're taking him. And how do I know you're acting in his best interests? I wonder if my mother would think so. She knows people who have to investigate if they think there's a question of child abuse.' I was on fire. The more I talked the angrier I became, and the more suspicious of Archimedes' intentions.

His face turned red and he stood up. '*Child abuse?* How dare you accuse me of such a thing? I cannot believe that I have to suffer such insults from an insignificant human who has no more intelligence than a gnat on my planet. Leave now.'

Something like an electric shock went through me when I heard those words. 'What did you say?' I stood up to face him.

His face paled and he took a step back. 'Nothing. Just that you're a young girl who does not know what she's talking about.'

'No, you said that I didn't have as much intelligence as a gnat on your planet. Where are you from, exactly?' I put my hands on my hips and took a step forward.

'Don't be absurd. That was just a figure of speech. You say the most ridiculous things.' He turned from me and started to pace the small room. 'I don't know why I have to put up with this. It's too much on top of everything else. The sooner we leave this place the better.' He seemed to be talking to himself.

'And where will you go?'

He waved an impatient hand. 'Alaska. Since Rion seems to have told you about our plans, I assume he told you that.'

'You're no more going to Alaska than you went to the Amazon. Rion admitted that wasn't true.'

Archimedes whirled around to face me. 'What do you mean? Why, we told you and your parents all about our trip when we came for dinner. And what a mistake *that* was. I had indigestion for days.'

I stopped myself from saying that perhaps he shouldn't have eaten or drunk so much. But I had some manners, and he had been a guest, however unwelcome.

'All you did was give us facts and figures and anyone could have gotten those online.'

He looked taken aback. And then he said, 'Why, of course we went there. I'm a photographer, of note, I might add. I travel all over the world.' He turned his back on me. 'I don't have to explain myself to you.'

This wasn't working. I couldn't get through to him. Maybe my approach was wrong. I tried again, using a soft and, I hoped, more persuasive tone.

'Archimedes, I don't mean to upset you. I'm sorry if I was rude. Please, tell me why you're doing this to Rion. He came to see me the other night and he was really upset. I'm his friend. I would miss him if he went and so would everyone else. Can't he at least stay here until he finishes year twelve? You know he's brilliant. He could probably get a scholarship to just about any university he applied to. Please let him stay. If you have to go away, fine, but Rion could stay with us. I know my parents wouldn't mind.'

Archimedes turned around and looked at me, his grey eyes no longer angry. Instead, he assessed me with a coolness that I found unsettling.

'It was a mistake for us to come back here,' he said. 'You care too much and so does he. I don't know how much you remember, but you'll forget again and it's best that you do. You have no need to worry about Rion. He will be fine. At the moment he's conflicted and is not thinking logically. But that will pass. Once he's back with his own people, he'll be happy again. He'll fulfil his mission and have a long and productive existence. You would be a selfish girl indeed if you tried to prevent this.'

He moved towards the door. 'And now you really must leave. You've accomplished what you set out to do, which was talk to me. You were successful in one way. It's made me realise all the more how important it is for Rion to leave. This place is not good for him. You are not good for him. How could you be?'

His words floored me. 'What do you mean? I'm his friend. I only want to help him.'

'If you really want that, you should let him go. He's intelligent and gifted, and why should he be tied to such an insignificant, unintelligent being such as you? He could have such rich and incredible experiences away from here. Staying in this backwater, what kind of life would that be for him? He's destined for greater things. You only make him weak.'

I felt the tears gather in my eyes. Was Archimedes right? Was I being selfish in wanting Rion to stay? His words affected me more than anything else that had happened recently. I had nothing more to say. I headed for the door.

Before I had a chance to leave, the front door swung inwards and Rion came into the hallway. He looked at me and then at Archimedes behind me.

'What's going on here?' he said.

'She was just leaving,' Archimedes said. He placed a not-so-gentle hand on my back, pushing me past Rion towards the door.

Rion put his own hand on Archimedes. 'Don't touch her.'

'I'm simply assisting her in leaving, you stupid boy. You're blocking the door.'

The three of us were crowded in the narrow hallway, with Rion and Archimedes glaring at each other. What had I done?

Rion looked down at me and said, 'Are you okay?'

'Yes, of course, Archimedes didn't do anything. I just came over here to talk to him.'

'There, what did I tell you?' Archimedes said.

'You'd better go now, Zoe. I need to speak with Archimedes.' Rion moved aside so I could leave.

I hesitated, not wanting to leave it like this. I looked up at him. 'Rion, I—'

He shook his head. 'Not now, Zoe,' he said. 'Just go, please. It's for the best.'

'You'll be okay?' I looked over at Archimedes, who gave an exasperated huff.

'Yes, I'll be fine. Don't worry.' He opened the door wide.

I nodded and left.

# Chapter Twenty-one

What the hell happened this afternoon? Why was Zoe here?'

'I knew something like this would happen and I was right, as usual.' Archimedes, looking grim, turned back to the lounge area and collapsed on the sofa.

I followed him, standing in front of him and folding my arms. 'What happened?' I repeated.

'She had some misguided idea that she could persuade me to let you stay here. And she was extremely rude, even suggesting such things as child abuse. Really? I still cannot believe it. You are well rid of these humans, I tell you.' He put his hand on his head and closed his eyes.

Zoe came here to talk to Archimedes? I was touched. She actually cared.

Archimedes opened his eyes. 'You'd better come home now, before she causes any more trouble. I don't know how you've lasted here for so long.'

'Archimedes,' I said, looking down at him and trying to control my temper, 'I am not going back. I haven't spoken to our supervisor yet. You promised to forward my request to him. Until I speak with him, I'm not going anywhere. And what did you say to Zoe to make her so upset?'

'*Her* upset? What about me? What about the wild accusations she was hurling about? What did you say to her? Have you told her the truth?'

'Yes.'

'Everything?' Archimedes was looking shocked.

'Yes.'

'So that's why she came here. That was most unwise of you, Orion. Now it will just be harder for her. I realised she knew something, but not everything. Surely you see the necessity of returning now.'

'You're wrong. She doesn't remember how she felt about me at all. If anything, she thinks I'm crazy.'

'And yet she came to see me. Interesting.'

'Why was she so upset when she was leaving?' I persisted. I hated to see Zoe like that and I was about ready to shake Archimedes.

'I imagine it was because I told her you were going back to your people. I never said where, by the way. I said you would be better off without her; she was no good for you and that she was being selfish in wanting you to stay.'

'You said *what*? How could you say something so insensitive and untrue?' Now I knew why there were tears in her eyes when she left. She must have been so upset when Archimedes said I'd be better off without her. Especially since she'd had only ever tried to help me. 'I have to go after her. I have to explain.'

'Sit down, Orion, and think for a moment before you do more harm.'

I sat down, not because I was convinced, but because I needed to hear more about what had happened so I would understand how to fix this.

'For millennia we've known it's never wise to get too involved with a host,' Archimedes said. 'Their lives, compared with ours, are so short and their wisdom so limited. Materialising in physical form happened so rarely that we never considered the consequences of that. You were an experiment, an experiment that went wrong. Zoe is not good for you. She clouds your thinking, makes you put emotions ahead of reason. That is not our way. And you are not good for her, either. She should be with one of her own kind. You know that, otherwise you wouldn't have asked me to take away her memories.'

I looked at him in stunned silence. Much of what he said was true. Harry was probably who Zoe should be with. Not me. But I had to correct him on one thing.

'Maybe I'm not good for her, but Zoe was the best thing that's ever happened to me. For all our knowledge and wisdom, we got one thing wrong. We've learnt far more from our hosts then they've ever learned from us. They share our lives with us and what do we give them in return? A few crumbs of knowledge when we feel the time is right, but never too much because we think they wouldn't be able to handle it. But you know what? *We're* the ones who can't handle things. We can't handle what it takes to be human—the courage and the defeats as well as the victories and, yes, the emotions. Our own emotions have been turned off for so long that we know longer value them. And that was our biggest mistake of all.'

Archimedes looked at me for a moment. Then he said, 'I see that nothing I say carries any weight with you, even though I'm older, wiser and your superior. I'm wasting my time here. I will pass on your request to meet with our supervisor immediately. It will be up to him what happens next. And if he does decide to let you stay, I'll ask him to release me from the job of being your guardian. I think that will be best for both of us.'

I was relieved, yet there was a small part of me that felt sad. I got on better with most of the humans I knew than with one of my own kind. But then a thought occurred to me. 'I wasn't expecting you this afternoon. Was there a reason you came?'

'Nor was I expecting to visit. But when you moved into this house, I put a forcefield around it so I would know if you had any intruders or unwelcome visitors. When Zoe went off the path and looked in the window, she entered the forcefield, so I materialised to see who it was and if you were in any kind of trouble.'

I was surprised that he had put so much thought into my protection. 'Thank you, Archimedes, it was good of you to take such care of my security.'

'I may not have been your idea of a perfect guardian, but I did my best,' he said stiffly. 'I have been here long enough.' He rose from the sofa, looking more tired than I had ever seen him.

'Goodbye, Archimedes,' I said.

He bowed slightly and closed his eyes. Within a second he had dissolved and the space before me was empty.

I knew he wouldn't be back.

I wanted to go to Zoe, but Archimedes' words did carry some weight with me. Zoe still didn't believe I was an alien, even though she had tried to help me. And maybe that was for the best. Knowing the truth would only confuse her more. She was better off with Harry and without me.

# Chapter Twenty-two

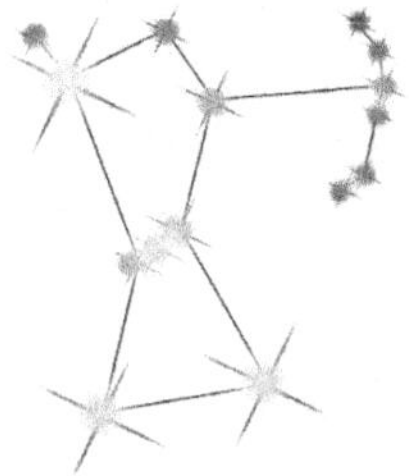

I made a face as I looked in the mirror. The dark circles under my eyes showed my lack of sleep and I felt as if my bones were made of lead. All night I had tried to put together the pieces of the puzzle that made up Rion. Nothing made sense, and talking to Archimedes had made it even more confusing. He'd said something about a planet, but then tried to backtrack fast. That tied in with the story Rion had told me. But aliens?

But what had hurt most were Archimedes' parting comments. Maybe I was being selfish in wanting Rion to stay, and maybe someone as ordinary as me wasn't good enough for him—not that we were together or anything— but Rion had said he wanted to stay.

Yet he hadn't got in touch with me last night. So what did that tell me?

When I went downstairs to grab a bowl of cereal, Mum glanced at me and said, 'Are you feeling okay, Zoe?'

I nodded. 'Just tired, that's all.'

'Don't push yourself too much with study,' she said. That was a first from Mum, her telling me not to study too much. Then she surprised me again by saying, 'Do you want to stay home today and rest? I can phone the school for you and let them know.'

'Goodness, where's my real mother? What have you done to her?' I said, getting the milk out of the fridge.

Mum smiled. 'Still here and just checking to make sure you're okay.'

'I'm fine, Mum.' Just for an instant, I felt like telling her everything that had happened. She would know what to do about the Rion situation and then I could let someone else handle it. I could give it to the grown-ups.

The moment passed. After all, I was nearly a grown-up, too, and Rion had asked me not to tell anyone.

'Okay, then,' she said. 'I'll be off. See you this afternoon.' She gave me a kiss on the head, picked up her bag and headed out the back door to the garage.

I poured the milk on my cereal and picked up a spoon. Rion and I needed to talk—today. I wanted to find out what was really going on. Maybe we could work something out.

But Rion wasn't at school, and he never answered my texts asking how he was. I was really starting to worry. Had Archimedes taken him away already?

After school, Harry insisted on walking me home, even though I wasn't much company.

'Okay, Zoe, so what's wrong?' Harry said after a few minutes.

'What do you mean?' I tried to act casually.

'You haven't been yourself today. You've hardly spoken to me or anyone else, and you look really tired. Something's obviously bothering you, so what is it?'

I sighed. I ought to know better than think I could hide anything from Harry. 'It's Rion,' I said.

'Oh,' was all Harry said, and he looked straight ahead. There was a lot of meaning in that 'oh'.

'No, it's not what you think. It's just … I think he's having some problems.'

'What do you mean?' Harry looked at me.

I knew I couldn't tell him everything, any more than I could tell Mum. But I had to say something. So I said what everyone would know soon know anyway. 'His uncle's taking him away again and I don't think he wants to go. In fact, I know he doesn't.'

'But that's really up to Rion and his uncle to sort out, isn't it? It's not your problem.'

Harry didn't get it. I tried to explain a little more. 'But don't you think it's strange that his uncle's taking him away again when they've only just come back? It's his senior year. Shouldn't he be allowed to finish it?'

'Well, his uncle's a photojournalist, isn't he? Maybe he has an important assignment and because he's Rion's guardian he has to take him along, too. After all, Rion can go to school somewhere else, or do correspondence school. He's smart enough.'

When Harry said things like that, they sounded so reasonable. Except I didn't believe for a minute that things would work out like that. Rion had been so upset. He'd said he was going back to his people; that he wouldn't be back. I knew he didn't want to go and I knew I didn't want to lose him.

Did that mean I was beginning to believe his story, which had sounded so crazy to me on Friday? I was confused and I didn't know how to explain it all to Harry, who was now looking at me with concern in his hazel eyes.

'Gee, Harry, I don't know. It's just that Rion seemed pretty upset when he told me about it.'

'If you're so worried about him, maybe you should speak to your parents. After all, he stayed at your place for a few months last year and they know him pretty well. They could speak to his uncle and see what's up.'

Again, so reasonable, but I couldn't just say to Mum and Dad, 'Hey, guys, Rion told me he's an alien and Archimedes wants to take him back to his people. So he's either crazy or out of this world, ha-ha. By the way, can you do something about it?'

Yeah, that'd go down well. And I definitely couldn't say any of that to Harry

'Yeah, Harry, you're probably right,' was all I said. 'That's a good idea.'

We walked in silence for a while.

As we were getting closer to my house, he stopped again. 'Zoe, I know you and Rion were pretty close last year when he stayed at your parents,' he said. 'Maybe you're not over that yet. Otherwise why would you be so worried about him?' He looked at me, his eyes questioning.

'I'm only concerned about him as a friend, that's all, Harry.' And I was.

'We're friends, too, and sometimes I wonder, could we ever be more than that? But Rion, he's always there, isn't he? He was last year and it seems like he is this year, too. Just tell me straight. Do I have a chance with you, Zoe?'

Talk about conflicted. I should've been able to give Harry an answer there and then, but I hesitated. I knew I cared about Rion, but for a little while I'd thought there could be something between Harry and me. Yet I knew the connection that I was starting to feel with Rion was something I'd never had with anyone else.

I knew all these things, but I couldn't find the words.

He kept looking at me for a few moments, and then said, 'Forget I asked.'

I could see, for a moment, that the old Harry was back, with all the doubts and insecurities he had lived with for years. I didn't want that to happen. He had worked so hard to be where he was. But I had to be honest.

'Harry, I don't know how I'm feeling right now. I do care about you. We've been friends forever. I'm just not sure what the next step is. But you're right about one thing. I also care about Rion, a lot.' Even as I said the words, I realised they were true. 'I don't want him to go, especially if he doesn't want to.'

'I think you've answered my question right there. You two last year, it was like there was this invisible bond between you that no one could break. It's still there, Zoe, whether you realise it or not. Maybe one day you'll figure out what you really want. I might wait, or I might not. But even if I do, I won't wait forever.'

He turned and walked back down the pavement. I wanted to call him to come back, but I didn't. Maybe Harry knew me better than I knew myself.

After dinner, Mum offered to take me out on a night driving lesson and, since it wasn't Dad, I said, 'I'm ready, right now. Let's go.'

I didn't want to give her time to change her mind, plus it'd be good to think about something other than the boys in my life for a change. We easily manoeuvred the city streets and I even had a go at parallel parking, which I aced.

As we drove towards home, Mum looked at me and said, 'How long has your grandmother been teaching you how to drive.'

'Honestly? You won't get mad at her or anything?'

'Yes, honestly, I know better than to get too mad at someone who owns a unit near Bondi Beach.'

'Okay, since I was fifteen, well, nearly fifteen.' I looked over at her and she smiled.

'Eyes on the road, young lady,' she said. 'Well, that's I relief. She started teaching me when I was twelve. She said that if she learned at twelve, then I could, too. Except that she lived on a farm in the country. And there was a lot less traffic on the suburban streets then, where she took me.'

I laughed. 'Did Grandad ever know?'

'Oh, God no, he would've had a fit. But Gran operated on a need-to-know basis when I was growing up. She never actually told lies, but she only told Dad the truth if she thought he could handle it. And, believe me, that was one truth my dad wouldn't have been able to handle.'

We laughed together, then Mum added, 'Not that I'm saying you should follow her in that regard. You know you can tell me anything, don't you, honey?'

She sounded so serious that I realised she knew there was something up with me. But I couldn't tell her what it was. Maybe Archimedes was right and I wasn't good for Rion, but at least I wouldn't betray his trust in me.

'Sure, Mum, I know that,' I said, as I indicated and turned the car down our street.

'So, do you want to talk?'

'Nothing to talk about, I'm fine, Mum, really,' I said, as I pulled into the driveway. I only wished it were true.

Later that night I texted Rion yet again: *Are you okay?*

I still didn't get a reply. Either he had already left and for some reason couldn't contact me (maybe Archimedes had taken his phone) or he just didn't want to. Maybe he felt I shouldn't have gone to see his uncle at all. It seemed all I'd done was make things worse than they already were.

The next day I went to school wondering if he would be there. He wasn't. I tried not to worry. I tried not to think: Will I ever see him again?

At lunchtime Lou said, 'Rion hasn't been here for a couple of days. He must really be sick. Have you heard from him, Zoe?'

I sensed Harry looking over at me. I just shook my head.

'I hope he's okay,' Lou said. 'He's such a nice guy. I mean, he explained that play to me so well last week. I totally got it.' And she actually blushed.

'I'd have to be dying to take that much time off school, especially this year,' Kerri said, as she opened a notebook crammed with neat writing. Her half-eaten lunch lay beside her.

'Rion's smart so I'm sure he'll catch up,' I said.

That night I tried not to look at my phone every five minutes. I just wanted to know what was happening. Then I could let it go. I could move on. I could stop asking myself questions.

Was he better off without me?

Was something wrong, or was he just keeping his distance from me?

I knew I would have yet another night without sleep.

# Chapter Twenty-three

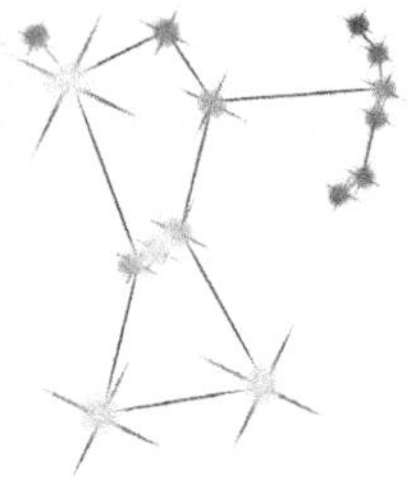

The translucent shimmering form before me appeared as a man with bright silver hair that curled around his forehead and the bluest eyes I'd ever seen. He looked neither young nor old but in his prime, even though I knew him to be over six thousand years old. I had never seen the physical form of my supervisor before, but if this was what he looked like before he left our planet and his organic body behind, he must have been one of the finest of our species. I knew his intellect and wisdom were far beyond mine.

And yet I'd asked for this meeting and he had come quickly. Archimedes hadn't been gone an hour. I realised my supervisor was granting me an incredible favour just by being here.

'Thank you for coming,' I said. I'd never realised before how crude and heavy my voice sounded. We hadn't needed speech before. Thoughts had been enough.

He bowed his head in acknowledgement. 'Your guardian said you wanted to speak with me.' Unlike mine, his voice was light and soft, like a whisper in my mind.

Overcome by his presence, it took me a moment to collect my thoughts. Finally I said, 'I was told you wanted me to give up this human form and return to our people.'

'I thought it best. Archimedes said this organic life was not good for you. Is that so? Have you wearied of living here?'

Archimedes, of course. Well, that was one statement I could challenge. 'No, I haven't. I haven't regretted my decision to be human, despite its ups and downs.'

'Perhaps I was hasty in giving you that choice. You know that if you continue in this organic form you'll live a normal human life and then die. Think carefully before you tell me again that you want to remain human.'

'I don't need to think it over. I'm sure of it. I would rather live one lifetime as a human than a thousand in my previous life.'

He was quiet for a moment and I felt my nerves stretched tight as I waited for his answer. Then finally he said, 'I see. You're still attached to your previous host, are you not? Zoe holds you to this life and that's why you're so reluctant to give it up.'

I thought for a moment and then said, 'Yes, that's true. But it's not the only reason.' I tried to explain. 'Can you remember back to when you were an organic? When you had senses? Do you remember the scent of flowers, the feel of a breeze, the taste of a sweet fruit? The touch of someone you cared about? We only experience life secondhand when we inhabit our hosts and those things don't seem to matter. But when I became human, all my senses were alive and I'd never felt so wonderful, so full of joy and happiness. I don't want to give that up. Given a choice, I wouldn't give it up.' My chest tightened, the breath caught inside it. Would he understand?

'My previous life was in another age,' he said, 'almost forgotten by what we call time. Yet now and then I catch a distant echo of that era. I once felt the soft lips of a beautiful woman and, yes, right then I would not have traded that moment for all the wisdom in the universe. But I was very young. And when I was called to my mission, to leave my home, my family and the woman I cared about behind, I was tempted to refuse.'

'Why didn't you?'

'She fell in love with someone else.' He smiled, but his eyes were sad. 'She made the right choice. That man was far more suited to her than I was. And I made the right choice, too. In the end it was better for both of us.'

I knew what he was saying. I thought of Harry, who was probably more suited for Zoe. But maybe Harry was the right choice for *now*. Maybe one day I would be the better choice. I had to hope. 'I understand your meaning, but I still want to remain human.'

He nodded. 'Very well, then, I have only one condition. You must enter a state of deep meditation for three Earth days. It will give you a chance to disconnect from all emotions, all ties with this world. It will, I hope, give you clarity of thought. You will have no contact with anyone, especially your former host, Zoe. If at the end of this time you're still resolved to remain human then I will grant you that wish. It will be irreversible. There will be no more chances. Your contact with us will be severed.'

He paused, as though giving me time to absorb his words. 'The rent on this house will be paid, and you will receive an allowance from a bank account set up in your name until you are, in Earth terms, eighteen. After that you will be completely on your own. In time you may even forget who you were, and even if others call you alien, that will no longer be true. Even more than before, you will be human.

'If, however, you decide to return to us, there will be no more contact with this girl. You will need time to be rehabilitated until you're ready for another host. That may take some time.'

'I understand.'

'I will not return. In three days' time, stand in this spot and speak your decision out loud. If you decide to stay, you will hear no more from us. If you decide to come back, your body will dissolve and your consciousness will return to us. You have been given a second chance to think about your future. Remember, there will be no others.'

I nodded. 'Thank you for allowing me this choice.'

His eyes became stern. 'Do not thank me. You may find cause, in the years to come, to curse me for giving you the right to choose. If you attempt to talk to anyone during your period of meditation, the choice will be rescinded. You will come back to us immediately. Think carefully, Orion, and choose wisely.' He slowly faded from my sight and the golden light that surrounded him disappeared.

Our people had long used meditation to help them remain calm and centred, although it had been a while since I'd practised it. But as I sat quietly on the bedroom floor, it came back to me. My breathing slowed, my mind stilled, and within a short time my emotions dissolved as if they had never been.

On Thursday night, my three days of solitary existence were over. My eyes slowly opened and I saw the glow from the streetlight outside spread across the bedroom carpet. Every day I had meditated for several hours, and in between had slept long dreamless nights. I was filled with a peace I hadn't known for some time. My supervisor was right. Meditation had cleared my mind. I knew now without doubt what my decision must be.

I went downstairs and stood in the quiet darkness. I said the five words that would change my existence forever: 'I choose to remain human.'

For a moment nothing happened. Then I became conscious of emptiness inside, an emptiness I knew would never be filled. I knew the alien within me had gone.

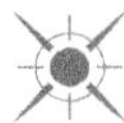

I wasn't really surprised when Rion wasn't at school again on Thursday. I knew I had to let him go, but knowing how was the difficult part.

I went home from school and straight to my room, not sure if I wanted to cry or punch something.

Opening my laptop, I researched the Spanish Civil War for my history assignment. I tried to read an article, but my attention kept wandering. Maybe Rion had had a good reason for not getting in contact with me these last few days. Even though I was annoyed, I couldn't stop the bubble of happiness that exploded inside me. He was going to stay.

It probably had something to do with Archimedes. I really didn't like that man.

I closed my laptop. It was no good. I couldn't stop thinking about Rion.

Later on, Mum and Dad went out for the evening to one of Dad's work functions.

'You'll be all right on your own, dear?' Mum said, as she popped her head in to say goodbye. Dad was behind her.

'What am I, twelve? I actually babysit, you know.'

'I know, just checking. You look a bit peaky. You might be coming down with something.'

'She's fine,' Dad said.

'I'm fine,' I said at the same time. We both laughed.

'We won't be late. Have a good night,' Mum said, and Dad finally got her out the door.

I was just debating whether to try studying again or watch something on Netflix when my phone rang. I looked down at the caller ID. It was Rion. My hand reached out to grab my phone from the bedside table and then I stopped.

Should I really jump out of my skin because he called—after three days of silence? Part of me was angry, but I was also worried. Maybe there was a good reason he hadn't called before. I reached out to answer it. Too late, it stopped ringing.

I was just about to pick up the phone to text him back when I heard a knock on the front door. I went downstairs to answer it with the feeling that I knew who it was.

I was right.

Rion stood in the doorway, dark hair skimming his eyes and looking unfairly great in a T- shirt that stretched across his broad chest. He was smiling that crooked smile that always seemed to get to me. I was so glad to see him. And relieved. But I tried to play it cool. After all, it had been three days.

'You didn't answer your phone. I thought you might not. That's why I didn't call until I was here. Hope you don't mind.'

'Hey,' I said, 'I thought you'd gone.'

His eyes met mine. 'No, I'm staying now.'

I resisted the very strong urge to hug him. 'Cool. Glad it worked out for you. You haven't been at school, though.'

'I know. Can I come in? I'll explain everything.'

'You've had plenty of time to do that. You didn't even reply to my texts.' Now that I knew he was okay, I was feeling angry and hurt at not hearing from him. I'd been seriously worried.

'I'm sorry. I don't blame you for being angry with me. I wanted to talk to you, but … I couldn't. Let me come in, Zoe, and I'll tell you everything.' His eyes were pleading.

I was always going to let him in, but I didn't want to make it too easy for him. I had my pride.

I sighed and opened the door wider. 'You can come in for five minutes only and then I've got to study.' I led the way into our lounge room and sat down on the sofa, folding my arms. He'd better have a good reason for his total silence the last few days.

He sat down next to me, which was not what I wanted at all. I should have chosen the chair. It was hard to think when he was so close.

'Okay,' I said, 'shoot.'

'Archimedes has gone,' he said.

That news was almost as good as knowing that Rion was staying, although I didn't share that thought out loud. 'Why haven't you gone with him? I thought you were leaving this week.'

'No, he's gone back to our people for good. And I'm staying here. I haven't contacted you for the last few days because my supervisor made it a condition before he would agree to my remaining here as a human.'

He still thought he was an alien. I didn't say anything. He was here, and that was all that mattered. The rest we could work out.

But my expression must have given me away, because he said, 'You still think I'm crazy, don't you?'

'No, I never thought that. I was worried about you, though.'

'I know everything sounds bizarre, but I'll try to explain it better this time. Will you at least hear me out?'

'Rion, what you told me last week in the boat, well, it was a shock at first, but some of the things that have happened lately have started to connect for me. Things Archimedes has said, the feelings I get when I look up into the night sky, flashes of memory that come and then go ... I don't understand it all, but I'm willing to keep an open mind. I want to believe you.'

'Good, that's start. What I told you last week was true. I'm not an ordinary person. I am from another planet. As I've said before, some of us gave up our physical bodies to become conscious entities so we could travel further in space. It also means our lifespans are much longer.'

'You look pretty physical to me,' I said, and blushed because I was thinking a totally irrelevant thought about what those strong arms would feel around me. Get a grip, I told myself.

'Yes, now I do, but for centuries, millennia, we inhabited humans. They were our hosts. You were one of them.'

'Yeah, you told me that.' It still felt a bit weird to think of that.

'When I materialised and couldn't change back, that was a big problem. But then they gave me the choice to become human. I thought that was it. But Archimedes decided that being human wasn't good for me and he wanted to take me back. That meant I would lose this human form and this life here. It was the last thing I wanted. I insisted on seeing our supervisor.'

'Your supervisor?'

'Yes, he's the leader of our space exploration team here. He's the one who ultimately decides everything. Anyway, he actually visited me, which was a huge concession, and he was much more understanding than Archimedes.'

'That wouldn't be hard,' I said.

Rion gave a half smile. 'No, it wouldn't. My supervisor agreed to allow me to stay, but on one condition. I had to enter a state of meditation for three days so I could clear my mind and make the right decision. During that time I was not allowed to have contact with anyone or the decision to stay would have been taken away from me immediately. I would've had to return to the mothercloud. I couldn't let that happen. Today, I gave them my decision. I am now completely human. My alien life is over and my people will never contact me again.'

It struck me that if this were all true Rion had made a huge sacrifice to become human. But the truth of it seemed irrelevant at the moment.

I looked up at him. 'That was a really brave decision to make, giving up your people and everything you were.'

Hope lit up his eyes. 'Does that mean you believe me?'

'I want to, Rion, I really do.' I was hoping that would be enough, but his face fell.

'You do think I'm crazy,' he said. 'I should never have let Archimedes take away your memories.'

We sat back on the couch, a dismal silence growing between us.

I closed my eyes. At times being with Rion felt so familiar. But the harder I tried to remember everything that had happened last year, the further those memories flitted away to the back of my mind.

I opened my eyes again to see Rion looking at me.

'Maybe in time, it will come back to you,' he said. 'But don't give up on me, Zoe. I've never met anyone like you. You've taught me more than any textbook I've ever read. You taught me how to live. Even if you don't like me, I want you to know that. If you ever need me, I'll be there. I'll always be your friend.'

I felt my eyes tear up. 'I do like you, Rion. But this is all too much. Sometimes I feel we *were* close, but I just don't remember it.'

He moved closer to me and I didn't move away. 'We were connected, Zoe. We knew and shared each other's thoughts for a short time. But it was only when I became human that I really felt close to you. Especially the first time I kissed you. Do you remember that?'

I felt his warm breath on my face and my stomach did a topsy-turvy thing, His dark brown eyes looked into mine.

I said in a breathy kind of voice, 'No, I don't remember.' But that wasn't totally true. I was remembering something.

'Do you want me to remind you?' he said, his face coming closer to mine.

I looked at him and felt like everything inside me was turning somersaults. 'Yes,' I whispered, 'remind me.'

He bent towards me and his lips brushed mine. I shivered, but I didn't move away. He pressed his lips harder and they moved slowly on mine. I still didn't move away. Instead, I let myself sink into that kiss and my arms found their way around his neck as he pulled me closer. I felt the warmth of his chest and his heartbeat.

A memory came back.

*We're dancing for the first time, and I can feel the steady rhythm of his heart. I'm surprised because I didn't think aliens had hearts. My fingers play with the soft dark hair that skims his neck.*

*A vision exploded in my mind, and I remembered the first time I saw him.*

*OMG, he's hot—for an alien.*

Butterflies danced like crazy in my stomach as his lips, so firm, moved over mine. Why couldn't I move away? Another memory, as warm as a spring day, washed over me.

*We're kissing for the first time. I didn't realise aliens knew how to kiss, at least not so well.*

Now, as Rion's kiss deepened, another memory came back to me.

*It's my sixteenth birthday and it's our last kiss. He's leaving and I don't know if I'll ever see him again. Tears fill my eyes.*

Rion lifted his lips from mine and looked deeply into my eyes.

'I remember,' I said softly. 'I remember everything. How could I have forgotten you, my incredible alien?'

Life doesn't always suck. Sometimes you get moments that are so epic you wish they could last forever. Feeling Rion's arms around me, and regaining all those memories of what we had shared together, made me so indescribably happy that it was almost scary. I'll never understand how I could have completely forgotten something that was so important to me, what Rion meant to me.

After all those months of hoping and wishing he'd come back, and then suddenly, nothing. Poof! All my intimate memories of him were gone.

Then, to have them all come back so suddenly, it felt surreal.

After that kiss (and maybe another one or two), we sat back on the couch, both trying to come to terms with what had happened to us.

Rion put his arm around me and I rested my head on his shoulder. 'When you didn't realise who I was, it was the worst feeling in the world,' he said.

'I remember you telling me once that feelings weren't considered important in your world,' I said, just a little bit smugly.

He groaned. 'Don't remind me of what I was like then. Having Archimedes around showed me how much of a pain I must've been in those early days, when I first materialised. No wonder you didn't like me then.'

'I got used to you,' I said. 'And you do scrub up well.'

He laughed. 'I've missed that.'

'What?'

'I don't know, the way you say things. You.' He tightened his arm around me and kissed the top of my head.

'I still don't really get why you let Archimedes take away my memories of you as an alien. I would never have told anyone, you know that. It would've been our secret. They'd think I was crazy. Heck, I thought *you* were.'

'But that's why I didn't tell you I'd decided to remain human in the first place. I might've looked like a human on the outside, but I was always an alien within. We were so different. I didn't think it was fair to burden you with a four-thousand-year-old alien. I wanted you to be free to choose.'

'That's funny. Archimedes said *I* would burden *you*. That I wasn't good enough for you.'

'Archimedes is an idiot. And if he was here right now I'd shake some sense into him.' Rion looked angry. '*You're* too good for *me*. That's the problem.' He brushed the hair away from my forehead and gave it a gentle kiss.

I let myself enjoy it for a few seconds and then I moved away from him and punched him in the arm.

'Ouch, what did you do that for?'

'For letting me go all those months thinking about you and missing you. So not fair, Rion. You didn't let me choose at all. You made the choice for me.'

A look of understanding came in his eyes. 'You're right. I never realised that before.'

'How would you feel if someone did the same to you, made a choice for you because they thought it was best? Especially if it was a choice you didn't want?'

He looked shocked. 'That's exactly what Archimedes did, and I was so angry with him I could've thrown him right back to the mothercloud, body and all.'

'But that's what you did to me. You took my choice away. I wanted to be with you, and when you went I was devastated.

So, you and I, we don't do that ever again, right? We make our own decisions.'

'You've taught me so much, Zoe.'

'I think it's time for you to teach me a few things.'

'Seems a funny time to bring up chemistry, but whatever,' he said, and smiled.

'Ha-ha. It's kind of like science, though. I'm thinking of compiling a study on how aliens kiss. But I might need some more fieldwork.'

He pulled me into his arms. 'I'm ready to volunteer.'

'I hoped you'd say that.'

It was only when we heard a key in the door that we realised we'd better bring our experiment to an end. Pulling away, I straightened my hair and Rion slid to the other end of the couch.

'Hi, Mum, Dad,' I said, 'look who's here.'

'Rion, how nice to see you,' Mum said. 'We haven't seen you for a little while. Stay for coffee. I've made some brownies.'

'They're only a little burnt,' I whispered to him.

He smiled at me and then looked up at Mum. 'Thanks, Mrs Brennan, I'd love to stay for coffee. It's good to be back.'

# Acknowledgements

So many people help in ways they don't realise in the life of any creative person. I have been blessed by being surrounded by those who understand and encourage me every step of the way and I am truly grateful to them.

To my husband, Rob, who, as an artist, has also trod this path; he has been supportive in so many ways. To my children, Ruth and Richard, who have always been there for me and have inspired me with their love, help and confidence in my abilities. Without Ruth, my website wouldn't exist, and without Richard, my understanding of technology would be even more limited.

And I cannot forget the person to whom I have dedicated this book: Jessie Beattie. She was a good friend to me throughout all the years since I first arrived in Australia. She read the first book in The Alien Chronicles series and was looking forward to this, the second one. Sadly, she passed away before it was completed.

I also owe a debt of thanks to the many writers who have helped me along the journey. A special mention must go to the members of the YA group, Write Links, who gave me critiques on sections of this book, and most especially to Tyrion Perkins, who gave me such valuable and detailed feedback on the entire manuscript. Thank you all for taking the time.

Another big thanks goes to the Romance Writers of Australia, a wonderful society that supports and helps all its members. Also, kudos goes to Anthony Puttee and his team at Book Cover Cafe, including my insightful editor, Penny Springthorpe. They all made the transition from manuscript to publication easier yet again.

And finally, to my readers, whose words of encouragement and enjoyment of the first book in the series, *My Alien*, have been reflected in their reviews and comments; they gave me the encouragement to forge ahead with *The Alien Within*.

# About the Author

Robin Martin has been a writer and a teacher for many years. Originally from Canada, she has lived and worked in several countries, but now lives just outside Brisbane, Australia. Writing has always been her passion, and in recent years she has written several novels and short stories for adults and young adults.

When she is not plotting stories, she loves reading everything from cereal boxes to long books that she can get lost in. She finds her inspiration in beach walks along the beautiful Queensland coast; an eclectic music collection that includes Mark Knopfler, ABBA and Mozart; and good coffee, without which she wouldn't be able to function. She and her family are also Star Trek fans, as is evident from The Alien Chronicles series.

Visit Robin at her website, www.robinmartinthomas.com, to find out about her other works and to sign up for her newsletter to receive updates on *Once an Alien*, the next book in The Alien Chronicles series.